All the Luck

KEVIN MCKEE

First Published in Great Britain in 2024

Dedication,

This book is dedicated to my late brother, Sean. Like Joe in the story, he faced and overcame great challenges in his life and became the wonderful and much-loved man his family and friends miss so much.

I also dedicate it to my darling wife Rosanne, who has supported me in so many ways and helped me to keep going in moments of doubt. I couldn't have done it without you, my love!

Some Guys

"Alright if I keep the radio on, mate?" asked the taxi driver.

"If you must," I muttered.

Well, I was paying him to drive, not to enjoy his stream of boring, middle-of-the road, middle-aged rubbish. He failed to take the hint and the radio stayed on, but I caught his frown at my tone in the rearview mirror. I resolved not to give him any tip at the end of the journey.

As the cab started off into the Fulham Broadway traffic, the radio began playing a song I knew. Appropriately, it was 'Some Guys Have All the Luck'. It also promised 'all the breaks'. This was one of those rare records of my parents' that Grumpus (that was my little kid's name for my paternal grandfather) liked.

"Do you know why some guys have all the luck?" Grumpus used to ask me whenever it was on the radio. "Because they make their own!" he continued, characteristically answering his own question.

That old pop song could be my theme tune, I thought, as I had just added another triumph to my recent list of achievements:

Got the job with a leading-edge management consultancy as their first in-house psychologist, check.

Quickly signed up their biggest client to pilot my groundbreaking new system, check.

Got flashy new digs for almost nothing, check.

Some guys do indeed have all the luck, and get all the breaks.

An hour ago, I had arrived at an address just off the Fulham Road, the location of my potential new flat share. I always arrive early for meetings to get familiar with the territory. In this case, I wanted to check out the neighbourhood I might be living in. After three months in London, my knowledge of the city's geography was still slight. I had not visited this area, so I had a lengthy wander around.

At first glance, it looked pretty decent: more independent shops and cafés than chains, amazingly, and away from the busy main road were some surprisingly quiet and leafy side streets. It seemed as if the flat – sorry, 'luxury apartment' – would be virtually on the noisy main drag, but that was London for you.

I stood outside the Arts Cinema that occupied the corner site at the address I'd been given. It was an impressive Art Deco building, built from creamy yellow stone with lots of curves and swoops in the façade. I'm generally not bothered about architecture provided the building does what it's supposed to do, but if you're going to have unnecessary garnish then Art Deco is better than most other frippery. I assumed that the flat I was vying for was tucked away on an upper floor or at the back of the cinema, but even so, what a location! I wondered, not for the first time, if this deal was too good to be true. At five hundred quid a month, the kind of apartment described by the letting agency had seemed outlandishly cheap. Cupboards in South Croydon were going for twice that! I was sure the inevitable catch would soon become apparent.

When I first contacted the letting agency two weeks ago, they had insisted that the price was correct but explained that the application process for the tenancy was unusual, to say the least. It entailed completing a long and complicated questionnaire, which formed the basis for a routine on-screen interview. Having cleared that hurdle, I was immediately invited to a Harley Street clinic, the following day for some tests and to answer questions about my recent health. There was also to be a lengthy interview with a fellow psychologist. I cleared my schedule and just hoped that jumping through these hoops would be worth it in the end.

Like the rest of Harley Street, the building I went to for my screening was grand yet wholly anonymous. Its internal décor was soothing and reassuringly expensive-looking. The reception staff greeted me warmly and took me to a small, blandly decorated room with a comfortable chair. No communal waiting room here! I guessed the kind of clients who usually frequented this place would be precious about their privacy.

A lot of people are nervous about being interviewed or assessed, but I relish the challenge. Given my education, I pride myself on being able to work out what even the most cunning interviewer is digging for and supplying the 'right' answers. I am never fazed by pressure tactics or challenging questions. Not that any of these featured in my conversation with Doctor Charles Rawnsley, OBE.

Rawnsley was a big name in assessing candidates for top-level executive roles. Ambitious as I am, I would never expect to be in front of him in that capacity. His presence suggested that no expense was being spared for what was, at the end of the day, just a flat share.

"Do come in, Joe," he said, in patrician tones doubtless refined by a public school and Oxbridge education.

He beckoned me into a large, book-lined study. The great man was silver-haired and distinguished-looking, impeccably dressed in a discreet, yet somehow stylish three-piece suit. What followed was a gentle, meandering dialogue that offered no clues about what I was being assessed for. We might have been two old pals meeting in a wood-panelled gentleman's club for a civilised chat over tea. The latter, accompanied by tiny, mouthwatering shortbread biscuits, was indeed served during our session. I took one biscuit to be polite, scrupulously observing my mam's instruction not to eat with my mouth open.

"It has been a pleasure to meet you, Joe," the good doctor said with a friendly smile at the end of our perplexing talk.

I'm sure he would have seemed just as benign if he had decided I should be locked away for the good of humanity. I had no idea what conclusions he might have reached but was slightly reassured when the assessment activities continued.

I was ushered into another room, this one a rather clinical environment, for my blood test. Then came the strangest element of the process. I had to put my left hand into some kind of scanner.

"What's this for?" I asked.

The nurse told me it was "Just part of the process." Odd, but at five hundred quid a month, bring it on.

I had presumably ticked whatever perverse boxes the Harley Street examination required, as the following day I had a call inviting me to view the flat and to be interviewed by the owner, who lived there himself. Meanwhile I had upgraded my aspiration list, yet again. One day soon I wanted to say of myself; "Wears an unfeasibly expensive hand-tailored suit, check."

A chilly March breeze had sprung up and I regretted not having worn a coat as I made the rather long walk from the tube station. Now, following my reconnaissance, I was freezing. I was also baffled about how to get into the flat. I could only see an entrance to the cinema itself which was shut. I peered through its windows but couldn't see anybody inside to ask for help.

I was getting a bit frustrated and also anxious about turning up late, so I wandered into the side street that formed the rest of the right angle that the cinema stood on. A few yards down I saw the narrow black and unnumbered door I would soon become all too familiar with. Embedded in the wall beside it was a tiny sign saying 'PRESS!' beneath a faintly illuminated button. Above that was what looked like a camera lens. The owner seemed the security-conscious type. I also noticed that there was no sign of a letterbox. Curiouser and curiouser.

Assuming that this was the door for the flat, I pressed the button as instructed. After a minute or so's delay, a voice bellowed, "COME UP!" through some concealed speaker.

Being used to direct communication, I pushed the door and confidently ascended the facing stairs ready to be a winner once more.

There was another anonymous door at the top of the stairs that clicked open just as I reached it.

"COME IN!" barked the voice I had heard over the intercom.

I pushed the door and walked into an entrance hallway far bigger than I would expect to find in a flat. I wondered if the apartment had the same footprint as the cinema had below; that would make it huge. Off to my right, an archway opened onto a large, well-appointed, fashionably monochrome kitchen-diner.

An East Asian man sat at the achingly chic dining table. He was typing on an oversized laptop and gestured in an abrupt way that made me stand still and keep quiet. I speculated about the likely cost of the dining table, which had a beautiful ceramic top, its surface decorated with swirling pink and grey clouds. This was supported by spider-like steel legs. Worth more than the flat I was currently living in? Quite possibly.

As I gazed around at the lavish fittings, I marvelled at the vast range of cooking equipment whose purpose I couldn't fathom. Maybe one day I too would have a flash home stuffed with high-tech toys I never used; another thing to aim for.

I surveyed my prospective landlord as he worked, trying to get some insights to help sell myself as his ideal tenant. The fact that he was sitting down with his head lowered limited my scrutiny. I reckoned he must be a good ten years older than me. Still, doing pretty well to have a pad like this in (almost) Central London by his late thirties. His body was lean and angular beneath a sweater that looked as elegantly high fashion as his home. Someday I'd have a jumper like that, though I didn't think I could rock that startling canary yellow.

After several minutes he slowly closed his laptop and looked up at me. He was wearing glasses that he took off, so presumably they were just for reading.

"Mister Dunne," he declared.

"Please call me Joe," I replied, extending my hand, which he ignored. He pushed out a chair with his foot, which I took as a sign I should sit down.

"I am Kang. From Korea; South. No nukes but good tech, HAHA! So, you want to share my flat, yes?"

I wouldn't describe Kang's tone as hostile, but he was certainly brusque. I was used to this from clients and indeed colleagues, so was not intimidated.

"I do," I responded. "I have my references here."

I pulled out my phone to show him the text and he waved it away with another dismissive gesture.

"No need. You been screened. Come and see accommodations."

Kang led me out into the hallway. We turned right and after several feet emerged into a vast light-filled living room. The source was a window running its entire length. Through the open venetian blinds, I could just make out the Fulham Road, but there was no hint of traffic noise.

"Quadruple glazing," my host explained, having followed my gaze. The room was furnished like I imagined the penthouse suite in a tastefully upscale Dubai hotel might be. Grey was much in evidence. The only splash of colour was provided by what seemed to be two pieces of abstract sculpture like giant mollusc shells in pillar-box red.

"You like?" he asked, again tracking my eyes.

"Er, yes; very Avant Garde," I replied.

"YOU know brand?" he asked in surprise.

"Sorry?" I was confused now.

He shook his head and laughed. "Avant Garde is brand of speakers."

I now noticed between the horn structures what must be a hi-fi but looked like the console of a starship.

"I demonstrate!" he proclaimed and dabbed at the smart watch on his right wrist. Instantly the room was filled with the sound of my second least favourite music: improvised jazz.

"Screech, screech, screech," went the saxophone. Grate, grate, grate went my teeth.

"Wow, really impressive!" I said in my best flattering but not totally sucking up voice.

"Not big fan, eh?" he said and turned the racket off. He stamped hard a few times on the lustrous wooden floor. "Quadruple sound proofing. They not hear my jazz, I not hear their blockbuster movie!"

He paused and added – rather wistfully, I thought – "No blockbuster, only things like Fassbinder retrospective. No boom or bang."

A closed door was set into the left wall as we faced the window.

"These Kang's rooms," he announced. "YOU – NOT – GO – IN!"

He paused after each word, like a teacher instructing a particularly dim pupil. He then led me back down the hallway where, opposite the kitchen, a door was slightly ajar.

He pushed it open and proclaimed, "This your room."

After the stark, modernist decor so far, I was relieved at the cosier style of 'my' room. Thankfully, the colour palette in here was not grey but muted shades of blue. It was a decent size with a double bed, armchair, tiny desk and chair. On the wall over the desk hung a medium-sized but modern flatscreen TV. Kang gestured to another door in the corner behind which was a small shower room with loo. Result! Surely, they'd left a zero off the end of the rent?

Our tour concluded with a grey-tiled cloakroom and a large cupboard or wardrobe beside the kitchen that I hadn't spotted on my way in.

As we returned to the kitchen, Kang asked "YOU LIKE?" in what I now took to be a habitually challenging tone.

I am no typical bashful Brit, afraid to haggle. I've gone toe to toe in negotiations and not shown it even if I wanted to grab the deal with both hands. "It might do," I replied.

He looked at me calmly for a few seconds, then barked out, "HAHA! I will tell what I expect of you."

I had already been informed by the letting agency about some of my landlord/flatmate's requirements. Once a week I would clean the whole flat, apart from Kang's room. I was baffled by this. Why not charge a market rent and be able to afford a team of cleaners daily? Fortunately, I am fairly house proud so not averse to a bit of dusting and scrubbing. I now discovered that I would also have to take down the refuse and recycling to a nearby collection point on the street each week. No problem: for the ensuite alone, I would personally have carried the bags all the way to the recycling centre on my back.

The rest of the expectations were more like rules: Put things away, keep the main rooms tidy, I could hang out in the kitchen and living room unless Kang wanted to have either one to himself, and so on.

"I work lot of time in my room," he reassured me. "Fine to have visitor, but no party and no girl or boyfriend move in!"

I was dying for my fiancée Liz to come and stay for a weekend to see my amazing new digs, but I assumed that would be okay.

My prospective landlord's final requirement was an odd one. I could not have any post sent to me at the flat. Instead, I would be given a PO number to use during the time I lived here. No other deliveries of any kind were allowed. There was a pickup/drop-off point for all the main carriers at the local newsagent that I could use. I considered momentarily if I should ask the reason for this restriction, but it was not that big a deal and I didn't want to come across as picky or awkward, so I agreed. Lucky I wasn't a pizza delivery fan.

Kang concluded with a loud and emphatic, "NO SMOKING!"

I'd never started, so that wasn't an issue, but I wondered if something in his tone or body language suggested regret? That's the trouble with a background in psychology: you never switch off.

Overall, I was happy with the arrangements Kang had stated but waited for him to suggest we had a deal. In fact, he spoke again, in a quieter and more confiding way.

"Of course, situations can change. Not all in our control. We can adapt, yes?"

This last question seemed almost a plea. I felt wrong-footed after all his previous abrupt and slightly eccentric comments and stuttered, "Er, yes…why not. Sure."

"GOOD!" he said with an air of finality. "You will move in next Monday."

As it was Friday now that seemed a bit soon, but five hundred quid, with an ensuite? All my bargaining tactics went out the window as I said, "Sure, that will be fine!"

That was the conversation over, seemingly. Kang turned away and went back into the kitchen.

"Bye then. See you on Monday," I said lamely. My host showed no sign of having heard so I let myself out.

I stood on the corner outside my soon-to-be new home thinking I would summon up an Uber when I saw the black cab. The prospect of escaping the March chill made up my mind. As I flagged down the taxi, I noticed on the list of feaure films and performance times that the Arts Cinema was showing a movie named *Fear Eats The Soul*. I shivered momentarily but put it down to the biting east wind and climbed into the cab.

Taking my lead as ever from Grumpus, I believed sincerely that we make our own luck. Most of the good and bad things that happen to us can be traced back to the decisions we make and the actions we take. Therefore, I mentally patted myself on the back for successfully navigating the perilous waters of the London rental market. Now, how could I use this abode upgrade to increase my status at work?

My reverie had distracted me so completely that I hadn't noticed when we reached Soho Square, my destination. Nor had I kept track of our route and rapidly increasing fare. (Should have got that Uber.) That reinforced my decision not to tip, and I imagined the cabbie flicking a surreptitious V sign at me as I walked away.

On The Greasy Pole

The rapid turnaround at Kang's flat meant I would reach the office well ahead of my hot desk slot. I had booked the corner one with the great views over Soho. It was normally the exclusive preserve of 'Established Consultants', but I was prepared to wait until it was free, even though nobody worth talking to would be in on a Friday afternoon. If I arrived early the thought of bantering with the common office drones did not appeal. Fortunately, my favourite coffee shop was down a side street off the square so I could both stay warm and top up my caffeine level as I waited.

Esperanza was a Soho institution that had endured despite the influx of many corporate coffee clones. Contrary to received business wisdom it had done so not by adapting but by remaining obstinately the same as it apparently had been since the early sixties. The decor was shabby, the seating uncomfortable and the service borderline offensive on a good day, but oh, the coffee!

I was lucky enough to nab a cramped perch at the infrequently cleaned counter. I caught the harassed barista's eye and projected my voice to register my flat white order.

My psychology degree had included a whole module on non-verbal behaviour. When it comes to influencing people the 'music and dance' make much more difference than the exact choice of words. To get the attention of a busy server your voice must be loud and forceful enough to get their attention. However, speak too stridently in somewhere like Esperanza and you'll be waiting until closing time for your drink. Who said psychology was a purely theoretical subject?

The barista nodded noncommittally. Experience told me that my drink would be a long time arriving, but I was in no hurry. Dropping into reflective mode, I remembered my first visit to the People People Inc office back in the autumn for my Assessment Day. The American company had taken a floor in one of London's swankier office buildings for their recently established UK business. They expected to grow quickly, so advertised for 'hip young gunslingers' to join the gang. I put in my application and endured a series of interrogations on Zoom over the next two weeks. These ranged from the short, by rote type at the beginning to the long and pretty aggressive cross-examination style as the field was whittled down. Eventually I was instructed to attend the final face-to-face assessment in London.

Boarding a super-early train down from Manchester, I had come determined to make sure I was the one they wanted. Most of the assessment consisted of the usual interviews and psychological tests. I was confident of being able to tell the assessors what I believed they wanted to hear on both.

The 'Pitch' was where I knew I could excel. People People Inc's main products were for Productivity Tracking. This meant using technology to keep an eye on what your employees did, wherever they were. It was huge in the States but had caught some flack in the more squeamish UK. In reality, this crude type of supervision has pretty much no positive impact on employees' productivity, but many companies find the illusion of control comforting.

My expertise was in giving employees the intangible things they needed so they produced more: listening to them, coaching them, using their strengths and so on. The research shows that those things really do lead to higher productivity and the increased profits that shareholders crave. I had no personal attachment to the softer side of management. If the research showed that driving people relentlessly and constantly controlling them increased profits, I'd have encouraged clients to those things. 'The highest productivity for the lowest cost' was the tag line for my independent consulting work. Blend it with Productivity Tracking, and People People Inc could take the UK by storm. I didn't mention that their tracking stuff was a load of self-defeating garbage and that my approach would soon be core to PPI's whole model. Foot in the door first.

I could tell the assessment panel loved my pitch. They tried their games to trip me up, but you can't kid a kidder, can you? The only part of the assessment process that made my tummy tighten in prospect was the Team Project activity. Groups are hard to predict; too many variables. Even though I'd studied and worked with group dynamics through university and beyond I knew I might need to flex all my mental muscles to make a good impression on the assessors.

There were eight candidates in the group, tasked with

sorting out a crisis with an imaginary client. Within a few minutes of the activity starting, I had taken a leading role with some assertive but supportive moves. Four of my rivals were going to be no competition, which left three to watch out for. One guy was forceful but a bit too pushy. By the midpoint of the task, he had overplayed his hand. A sparky young woman with some good ideas seemed like she might be trouble but when she started throwing jargon around, I knew she was toast.

I would have been the standout candidate if it hadn't been for Aretha. Yes, that really was her name, so instant points for memorability. She also somehow looked like she could belt out "R-E-S-P-E-C-T" with no problem. Her voice had a rich and almost melodious quality, reinforced by fluid movements and gestures. I had learned to deliver my ideas with impact but she was clearly a natural. To make matters worse, she was just that bit smarter at influencing the others than I was. I could have tried to take her on for leading the group, but something told me I would lose. Still, my back-up strategy of acting like a loyal lieutenant worked well enough. I just hoped that my pitch had put hers in the shade.

The Assessment Day finished with feigned hearty thanks from People People Inc's UK Managing Partner. They would contact the successful candidate within twenty-four hours. Presumably the rest could draw their own conclusions.

I saw the other candidates waiting for the lift and couldn't stand the thought of travelling awkwardly down with them so loitered until they'd gone. Aretha hadn't been part of the waiting group, but she appeared just as I pushed the button for an elevator myself. We stepped into the lift together. She pressed 'G' then turned to me and said, "Smart work in the group activity. I guess they might offer you a job."

I couldn't work out her angle so played the ball back to her. "I was thinking they might offer it to you."

"They did," she replied casually.

My heart sank but she followed up with, "I turned it down."

I was simultaneously pleased and confused, and a slightly too strident "Why?" came out of my mouth.

"I'm just using today as a warmup for a job I actually want." She replied nonchalantly. "These guys are all brain and no heart. Not my scene at all."

The lift whispered its way to the ground floor and Aretha walked out into the lobby, then said over her shoulder, "You should fit right in."

When the call came the next day to invite me onto People People Inc's elite team, I had a nagging sense of being second best.

First reserve I might have been, but to me People People Inc was my chance to progress to that 'next level' that people in the sports world bang on about. I'd done pretty well as a freelance consultant since leaving uni five years ago, but I needed a bigger stage to strut on. Sacrifices had to be made, of course. No way could Liz and I afford to keep the flat in Manchester on. She'd had to move back in with her parents for the time being. It was a pain that I was instructed to start in London just before Christmas, resulting in tearful farewells at the station. I assured Liz it would all be worth it in the long run.

My plan was for us to get a place in London once I became an 'Established Consultant' at People People Inc with some security and a hefty pay rise. I targeted myself to achieve this by the summer, then Liz could look for a school down here to teach at for the new academic year. Everything would be settled in time for our long-awaited wedding in October. She wasn't crazy about the deal, but I had talked her round as always.

People Who (Don't) Need People

My espresso had taken even longer to arrive than usual, so I ended up chucking the boiling hot coffee down my throat then jogging around to the office.

My employers expected their consultants to be mostly out at clients or working from home (having their productivity tracked, of course), so visiting HQ was still something of a novelty for me. The bland building reception was staffed by generic outsourced contractors whose faces changed regularly. People People Inc's own reception on the fifth floor was much snazzier. Two young Armani-clad Welcomers, one male, one female, stood behind lecterns, clutching iPads. Their main role was to fawn over clients as soon as they stepped from the lift. The same devotion was accorded to our own senior managers. I, on the other hand, received the slightly resentful stare reserved for all others, as if I had rudely interrupted the Welcomers' modelling careers.

I managed to catch the eye of the male Welcomer

(Sebastian?) and asked him if my hot desk was available.

"Not really," he replied. "Client conference call over-running. You could have one of the other desks?" he suggested, with take it or leave it aloofness.

"I'll wait," I responded.

My situation was obviously a matter of supreme indifference to Sebastian but he pointed to the far wall and said with a smirk, "Why don't you take a seat and enjoy the show?"

This was a mocking reference to the TV screen facing the well-upholstered reception chairs. It was showing, on a continuous loop, highlights of the People People Inc UK Retreat the previous month, which I had missed due to having flu. This annual event was the only time that Luke Peters, our esteemed leader, graced the UK team with his presence.

At first, I had been frustrated at missing the Retreat. The flu knocked me out for nearly two weeks at what seemed like the worst possible time. But as I reflected afterwards, it was really a lucky break. Instead of meeting the Big Boss as a callow rookie I would see him next year as an Established Consultant with an eye-catching client success to flaunt; much more like it!

As I sat down, the video had reached the point where Luke was giving his inspiring pep talk to the consultant team. The setting was the rococo-styled ballroom of the grand country house that had hosted the conference. The man himself, a tanned and expensively coiffured forty-something, sported a black T-shirt emblazoned with a grinning red skull and the words, "Yay though I walk through the valley of the shadow of death I shall fear no evil for I am the meanest sonofabitch in the valley."

Standing beside but discreetly behind him was our UK Chief Executive, Julia Reeves-Harding. Her T-shirt featured a stylised picture of two vultures sitting on a telegraph wire. A speech bubble emerged from one's mouth saying, "Patience, my ass; I'm gonna kill something."

I had already tormented myself by watching the retreat video several times and I could quote verbatim everything Luke had said. At this point it was: "Some people define a consultant as someone who borrows your watch to tell you the time then sells it back to you for a thousand bucks. I disagree – that's way too cheap! Let's value what we do, team, and be ready to demand **top** dollar every time. Because we're worth it."

I was planning to do exactly that when the pilot of my new Productivity 2.0 system ended with a delighted client prepared to pay a handsome premium for a full roll-out in their business. Just wait till they get a taste of Joe Dunne and experience stuff that actually worked!

"It's ready," the Welcomer said in my general direction.

I took that to mean that my hot desk was free and went through to claim it. As I walked across the floor, at intervals the walls featured framed posters expressing People People

Inc's company values. I passed: "Lunch is for Wimps," "I'll rest when I'm dead," and a larger, uncaptioned poster showing Leonardo DiCaprio in *The Wolf of Wall Street* grinning at the world as he exploited it. I admired the company's ruthless culture, but did they have to be quite so cheesy about it?

A few of my colleagues – all looking rather glum, I thought – were making their way out after the conference call, but apart from them I seemed to be the only person on the whole floor. This place really was dead on Fridays. As I approached my designated hot desk, I realised that, sadly, that wasn't quite true…

The Retreat video had included a moment when Julia had introduced the latest member of "our high-performing UK team." This was apparently a "superstar in the making" whom she had talent spotted on her last visit to our headquarters in California. She had personally negotiated with Luke for this genius to have a placement in the UK business.

Our new colleague looked about ten but was apparently eighteen, though still described as "a prodigy". His name was Chuck Humphries Junior. (His parents must really have hated him to saddle him with that handle.) His background fitted with People People Inc's technology roots. Indeed, Chuck had adopted all the classic tech bro affectations down to the ludicrous shortness of his trousers.

No protracted selection process had been applied to the good Chuck. Julia shared with most senior managers I'd ever met a belief that 'she could pick 'em' despite all evidence to the contrary. Thus were so many square pegs unsuccessfully hammered into round holes across the world. When I once viewed Chuck's LinkedIn profile it was a riot of overblown tech jargon and unsubstantiated achievements. Truly, it is not what you know but who you know.

There was no indication of what Chuck's role would be apart from 'troubleshooting'. This was the cause of great consternation in the 'high-performing team,' in which everyone was constantly obsessed with where they stood in the pecking order.

Chuck and I had taken an instant dislike to one another the first time we met a few weeks back. I think he started it when on introduction he called me "Joe Dumb."

"It's **Dunne**," I corrected him at once, to which he responded, "Well, I guess we'll see, huh?"

As I neared the coveted corner hot desk cubicle, I saw that someone was already in it, lounging back in the chair. To my dismay, I saw the annoyingly affected floppy hair of my nemesis.

As I approached Chuck I said loudly, "You've made a mistake here. I have this desk booked."

The incumbent slowly pushed his chair back and turned to face me, still in a reclining position. He grinned and said, "Well, if it ain't me old mite Joe Dumb. Wot a luverly surprise, corblimey."

When I was a little kid one Christmas when Dad was

away for work, Mam had tried to cheer me up by sitting with me to watch one of her own childhood favourite movies, *Mary Poppins*. Although I thought it was quite old-fashioned, I enjoyed Julie Andrews in the title role, admiring her perky irreverence. I was less sure about Dick Van Dyke as her friend Bert. His gurning performance of 'It's a jollee 'oliday wiv Muree' quite disturbed me.

"Why is that man talking funny?" I asked innocently.

"He's pretending to be from London," Mam replied.

"Is that how people in London talk?" I enquired.

"Not really, Joe," she said, "He's just not very good at accents."

Chuck had possibly based his piss-taking English accent on Bert's mangled Cockernee and, boy, was it annoying!

"So, are you going to get out of that seat and let me use this desk?" I asked, controlling my irritation at least for the moment.

He pretended to consider the options and then said, "Lummy, oi don't fink so, guvnah!" He then sat up and continued in his own, American accent. "You are low on the totem pole, Joe Dumb. You think your so-called 'Social Sciences' with all those voodoo statistics that don't mean squat are gonna help you get ahead here? Dream on, sucker. I wouldn't get too attached to the corner desk if I was you. Soon they won't even be letting you in the building."

Chuck had picked the wrong candidate to try his Imposter Syndrome schtick on. My self-belief, conditioned by years of tough coaching by Grumpus, was unshakeable.

I upped the volume and firmness of my voice as I said, "You do realise that Julia herself introduced the hot desking system here? She's a stickler for the rules too." As I said this, I surreptitiously put my phone onto 'record' mode.

"Hah!" Chuck bit back. "You think that stuck-up bitch will last much longer than you? Luke only recruited her for her contacts, and once we've taken over those she'll be gone, gone, gone. I doubt the know-nothing airhead will even see it coming."

I hadn't realised he resented Julia so much. Talk about biting the hand that feeds you. I wanted to keep Chuck ranting, so I shook my head vigorously to provoke him. That's all it took.

Chuck continued his diatribe. "Once she's been kicked out, I'll be taking over that big office of hers. First thing I'll do is have the place fumigated! Then I'll get rid of all that prissy crap she's stuffed it with and redecorate. Plenty of original Marvel movie posters and a big ole juke box in the corner. All my favourite techno bangers playing every day."

Yes, Chuck was obsessed with my number one least favourite kind of music! Give that man a prize.

He seemed to have run out of invective, so I flicked

'record' off. What I had should be plenty to get him fired when the time suited me.

I decided to let him have the corner desk today rather than waste valuable work time, but before I went I decided to impart some words of wisdom.

Looking down at Chuck, I said, "We much-maligned social scientists have a theory named cognitive dissonance. You might want to look it up. It shows that when someone has made a bad decision, they feel obliged to defend it, even to double down, but over time the effect tends to fade. Now, Julia is many things, but she is not stupid, and I predict that someday soon she will realise that you are about as much use as an inflatable dartboard. When you are carrying out your stuff in a black bag I'll be standing there to say, "Cheerio, me owld cock sparrer!"

I left Chuck sputtering "bullshit!" in my wake and sat down at a desk as far away from him as I could get. I felt that our battle had ended in a draw but, little did my opponent know, I was now tooled up to win the war.

So, to work. I was ahead of schedule in preparing for the forthcoming pilot project, but there was no harm in tightening the screws a bit more before we launched it. I connected my laptop and saw that I had just received an email from Julia, no less. Maybe my day was going to get even better...

It wasn't.

The message read:

"Productivity 2.0 pilot put on pause. We need to talk next week. My PA will send you an invite."

This was classic Julia style: no greeting or sign-off and strictly on a what you need to know basis. Experience had taught me to expect no sympathy as the person whose first major project had just ground to a halt, but to be left dangling until her assistant got round to finding a window for me? Gee, thanks a lot!

Having basically no work for now, I decided to pack up and go home. Doubtless my Productivity Tracking Checker would send me a Yellow Card for wasting office resources, but in the circumstances, I reckoned I could get it rescinded. Too many Yellows or, even worse, a dreaded Red Card would lead to immediate bonus reduction, so they were not to be taken lightly.

As I walked back through reception, the Welcomers were busy discussing their weekend plans. They looked up briefly to check I wasn't anyone important, then resumed their conversation. I'd always promised myself that on the day I took over from Julia as CEO – no more than eighteen months hence, in my fevered imagination – I would fire those two chuckleheads if they were still working here.

I grinned at the thought and shouted, rather loudly, "Have a wonderful weekend, you two!"

I doubt they even registered it.

Maddy

I felt I would never get used to travelling by tube. I loved Manchester's trams, but extended periods underground just didn't do it for me; nor did changing lines and using those horrible escalators. I suspected that, like learning a foreign language, once you passed a certain age without having experienced it you would never be fluent. Some part of the brain had failed to develop properly and the whole process would always be onerous. I particularly hated trips with multiple changes, so my impending journey to Rayners Lane filled me with gloom. All three trains I had to take were packed with Friday afternoon slackers on their way home. I felt slightly embarrassed to be one of them, so I was in a really bad mood as I emerged from Rayners Lane Station to find that the keen westerly wind had been joined by relentless drizzle.

I was decidedly soggy when I got home, which was a tiny flat above a bank on Rayners Lane High Street. Entry was via a back door accessed with the aid of a rickety metal staircase unlikely to win any health and safety awards. It was cramped and located in the outermost bit of Outer London. Nevertheless, I was eternally grateful to my friend Maddy – known as Madhura to her doting parents – for letting me stay there. Otherwise, I would probably have spent my early months in London freezing in a hostel given People People Inc's pay rates for 'Qualifying Consultants'.

As I towelled myself off and changed into dry clothes, it occurred to me that I needed to let Maddy know I would be moving out in a couple of days. She knew I was idly looking for somewhere much closer to the centre but, like me, she probably thought it was wishful thinking. I doubted that she'd miss the small amount of rent she reluctantly accepted from me, but I knew she didn't like the flat to be empty while she was away. I picked up my phone to send her a message suggesting we speak but spookily there was one from her suggesting a call that evening.

I always looked forward to talking with Maddy. Unlike me, she didn't take life that seriously. Right now, she was enjoying an extended break as a ski instructor at some high-class resort in Austria, having taken a sabbatical from her never-ending Dentistry degree. She'd had to re-sit the second year, which she explained to me by saying, "I had a problem with the practical, Joe. It's the bit where you have to keep a straight face while telling the patient what you'll be charging them." Now, after completing year three, she had wangled twelve months off to spend winter on the slopes and summer at the beach as a bodyboarding coach. That was typical of Maddy's charmed life. (Some gals have all the luck?) Despite my usually competitive nature, I didn't begrudge her any of it. If there was anyone in the world who I would call a friend, it was Maddy.

I had learned in my formative years to keep my circle of

friends a very exclusive club. Since the age of twelve, I had spent some time every year with my grandfather on his boat on the Fylde coast, a particularly windswept bit of the Lancashire coast. Being a peninsular it has a cut-off, rather insular, feel that suited Grumpus perfectly. I thought of my trips there as extra holiday, but to Grumpus I was an unpaid deck hand who did as I was told. He would always ensure that I visited when he was scraping the boat's encrusted hull. This was hard labour for a little kid, but I never complained. His direct, expansive conversation was a blessed relief compared to my awkward, usually brief, interactions with my own father. My receptive mind hungrily consumed Grumpus's morsels of wisdom.

One of his favourite topics was friendship and how overrated it was.

"You finding those barnacles hard to scrape off, lad?" he would begin. "That's what people are like. They'll cling to you and slow you down if you let them. You only need one or two good friends in this life. Keep the rest at arm's length. If they're any use to you, take them for what they're worth, then move on."

I had carefully logged this advice and stuck with it ever since. Maddy, however, was no barnacle.

It was Freshers' Week, an astonishing eight years ago, when I first met Maddy. The Freshers' Fayre was an event where all the university societies tried to recruit members from the gullible first-year population. We were standing next to each other while the head of the 'Creativity Crowd' droned on about innovation and new perspectives. Joining his group would allegedly free up my mind and result in a cascade of radical ideas and breakthrough thinking. At this point all that I was experiencing was a slight headache. He was showing a series of slides illustrating current trends in disruptive technologies when the cool South Asian girl standing next to me yawned expansively and muttered, "Who knew creativity could be **so** boring?"

I responded with faux enthusiasm: "Well, maybe this is just a deceptively counterintuitive way of getting us excited about creativity!"

"Yeah, total inversion. Whoo hoo!" Maddy shouted hysterically.

The Creativity Crowd supremo stopped and tutted, which made us both giggle. Still tittering, Maddy asked me, "Fancy a beer?"

"Provided it's served in a Suprematist teapot," I replied creatively.

From such humble beginnings a lasting friendship grew. Maddy was only mildly disparaging about my Psychology studies from her lofty perch as a Human Biosciences undergraduate, the first of many disciplines she was to embrace and then cast aside. Right from the start she made it clear that she was gay and that I would just have to admire her platonically. "On the plus side, I'm in a great position to vet your prospective girlfriends and guide you away from the crasser habits of your sex."

Maddy would often tease me about how I "talked like a grandad." To reinforce the point, she puffed on an imaginary pipe. I explained that my own grandfather would never tolerate my using slang or exaggerating my northern accent.

"You'll never get anywhere in life unless you speak properly, lad. Talk like a slum kid and you'll end up as one."

Maddy looked at me pityingly and said, "Luckily for you, Joe, I am the all-seeing Mystic Madhura and can discern the fun young guy beneath your crusty exterior."

I positioned myself as comfortably as possible on Maddy's lumpy sofa with my iPad on her rickety coffee table. Her idea of upcycling was to scavenge some worn-out piece of tat and just use it. What happened to the 'up' bit? A vision of Kang's immaculate designer furniture swam before me, but I dismissed it to concentrate on connecting with Maddy on her ancient and well-travelled tablet in Austria. At least the broadband at Maddy's resort was reliable, so provided that the dodgy signal at her flat held on we could have a decent catch-up.

It was really nice to see her face, which was tanned a deeper brown than usual and also a bit leaner.

"Hi, Joe. How's the King of Consulting?" she asked.

"Uneasy lies the head that wears a crown," I replied.

Her expression changed to one of sympathy; she was probably the only person I knew where I believed that to be completely genuine. "Aah, how come?"

I told her the sorry tale of my afternoon and felt a little better after a good listening to.

My turn to ask a question. "And how is the Empress of the Slopes?"

Up until a couple of days ago, very well, it seemed, but there was obviously something less glowing to report. To stave that off and my probably unwelcome news about moving out, I changed tack.

"Have you found the girl of your dreams there?"

She replied, "A couple of contenders, Joe, but none quite dreamy enough."

Maddy didn't seem too downhearted; she always seemed to enjoy the thrill of the chase more than the catch itself. "By the way, have you read my favourite book yet?"

Maddy had bought me a copy of *A Suitable Boy* two years ago on the solemn promise I would read it.

"Not yet, but it looks like I might have plenty of time to get stuck in now."

She tutted. "Please do so, Joseph. You might learn something useful. Also, it will prepare you for when I write my own take on this subject, 'Unsuitable Girls'!"

I laughed. "Sounds more my kind of thing, Maddy. Can't I just wait for that?"

I was about to tell Maddy about my new flat when she preempted me with, "Look, I'm sorry, Joe, but I'll need the flat back very soon. There's some kind of flu ripping through the resort so it's closing pretty much straight away. I'll be coming back at the start of next week. Don't worry about the short term. I can stay with my folks until you find somewhere else."

I was glad to be able to put her mind at rest by sharing my news. She was fascinated by the story of Kang and his unfeasibly cheap luxury let.

"I hope his intentions towards you are honourable, Joe?"

"Ha ha," I responded. "If not, I'll come to you for some tips."

We talked enjoyable trivia for a while and speculated about the flu bug; how serious could it really be? I caught sight of the time on my screen and, appreciating Maddy was an hour ahead of me, let her go off for a late drink in the bar.

"The girl of your dreams could be sitting there right now," I advised. "You never know."

She replied, "And when I find her, don't forget you're going to be my 'Mate of Honour'. Also, don't worry about work. Life has something better waiting for you, sunshine."

On my last night at Maddy's I had a strange and disturbing dream. I couldn't remember much detail when I woke up but it involved lots of people I knew, including my parents, Maddy, Liz and, surprisingly, Kang. I have a feeling Grumpus made a posthumous appearance too, shaking his head at me for some reason. Everyone was rushing around frantically and shouting at me. They seemed to want me to do something but I couldn't understand what they were saying. Oh, and they were all wearing medical face masks, which did nothing for their intelligibility. I vaguely recalled trying hard to understand them; just slow down and stop shouting! They were starting to make me feel anxious so I turned my back on them all and walked away but I tripped and stumbled. I began falling, and then I was awake.

I am by no means superstitious, but I lay trembling for a long time after the bad dream. Thankfully, my native cynicism eventually came to the rescue. The call with Maddy, news items about the flu spreading from Asia showing everyone masked up, my impending move, etcetera, etcetera. Sometimes, Herr Freud, a cigar is just a cigar.

KYPRO

My first week living at my new digs was a mixed experience. I loved my room and enjoyed the small but perfectly formed ensuite. Kang seemed to spend most of his time in what I assumed was a substantial office connected to his bedroom, so I often had the run of the kitchen and living room. The man himself would appear in the kitchen from time to time and make himself a coffee using a barista rig that would put Esperanza's to shame. He scarcely looked at me and responded to any questions monosyllabically. He never offered me a drink but by watching him I at least worked out how to make my own. It seemed that my sparkling repartee was not a feature my landlord wanted to enjoy.

I was constantly impressed by the no-expense-spared quality of the apartment. I even found myself running my hands over the beautiful and varied wooden surfaces. To my embarrassment, Kang walked in while I was stroking a cabinet in the living room that had the most sumptuous burr finish.

"HAHA!" he announced himself. "You have good taste!" He retrieved his phone from the coffee table and added, "All my wood is sustainable!" then stalked out. At least he hadn't accused me of being a timber fetishist.

Having no project work left me languishing with unexpected time on my hands. As a self-confessed workaholic, my drug of choice had been cut off. Not wanting to replicate my furniture fondling faux pas, I decided that some outdoor time would be a useful distraction. Off I went to explore my new neighbourhood. All the signs were good: it was indeed a buzzing area full of little cafés, restaurants and galleries. There was a park just a mile down the road and over Battersea Bridge.

I must give it to the teeming metropolis: while overrated in many ways, it couldn't be beaten for parks. Battersea Park was a classic, full of life and stuff to see. I was particularly impressed by the Peace Pagoda, a Japanese Buddhist donation to commemorate the atomic bombings of Hiroshima and Nagasaki. It looked incongruous but was oddly moving and made me thankful I lived in a place and time free from global disaster. Yeah, maybe luck was a thing.

I've always liked a boating lake, and the one in Battersea Park was huge. When Liz came to stay, I would impress her with my rowing skills and maybe we'd enjoy a picnic on some shady bank. I stopped suddenly as my inner Grumpus began to chide me for daydreaming. I needed to keep my momentum up, not moon around! I set off at a brisk pace to get back to the flat and do some contingency planning. Nearby some guys were playing football, a game I unreservedly detested. They seemed irked when the ball rolled over to me and I just strode away instead of kicking it back; I am nobody's ball boy.

By the time I crossed the bridge heading for Kang's, the late afternoon had shaded into evening and a chilly wind blew away any premature thoughts that spring had arrived. I found myself feeling reluctant to go straight back to the flat. *Fear Eats The Soul* had a poster that seemed more ominous every time I passed it. The two strange people it depicted seemed somehow ever more desperate in their embrace. Also, the prospect of being ghosted by my landlord hardly drew me in.

On impulse, I went into a self-consciously hip bar on the corner opposite the cinema. The sign on its industrial-style metal door proclaimed its name as 'KPYRO'. The drinks list explained that this was a Russian word for 'Awesome'. Really? Well, any port in a storm, as Grumpus might have said.

As I would have expected, the place was full of designer-clad clones. The guys all had those fashionably wispy beards and the gals sported 'natural' looking hairdos that probably took half a day in the salon to achieve. I grabbed the last vacant stool at the bar and overpaid for the Craft Beer of the Month, *Lobotomiya Frontal*, which turned out to be some kind of stout. I took a sip and immediately wished that the brewers had spent more time perfecting their product than making up a daft name for it.

Two guys sitting next to me at the bar were having a slightly drunk and over-loud argument about the flu epidemic that Maddy had mentioned, and that was starting to dominate the news.

"Storm in a teacup, bro!" opined one, slopping his neon bright Happy Hour cocktail onto the bar. "Now Boris has got Brexit done this country should be forgin' ahead and not lettin' some bug slow us down."

His mate, who looked a couple of drinks ahead in the let's-fall-off-our-seats stakes, went off at a tangent. "I've heard it's a bioweapon that the commies are tryin' out. They're using it to attack our immune systems cos their own are..." he struggled for *le mot juste* – "immuner!"

As I looked sideways at the two buffoons, I quickly assessed them. I estimated they were both a few years over the typical age of the other patrons. Though they styled themselves like the rest of the crowd, complete with obligatory wispy beards, they still looked out of place. Everyone else was so busy looking at each other without trying to show it that they weren't doing much drinking, while these two chugged down beer and cocktails with abandon. Although they were seated, I could tell that one guy was a hulking beast and the other looked like a breath of wind would blow him over. Their dialogue reflected their physiques. The hulk would make overly loud assertions and his diminutive mate would vigorously agree, often adding an absurd non sequitur. Some psychologists call this behaviour 'script-driven'. I call it damned tedious.

After a few minutes, I had exhausted the limited delights of people watching. I necked the last of my outrageously expensive and absurdly named drink before trudging home.

The Home Front

In the evening I had a Zoom call with Liz. I had become used to this tech through work, but being less familiar with it she found it artificial and limited.

"One day this could be everyone's main way of communicating," I had recently tried to reassure her.

"That's something to look forward to," she had tartly replied.

I had met my fiancée three years ago at a Smoke Fairies gig in Manchester. Nobody I knew liked folk music, which was one of the reasons I enjoyed it. Is there anything duller than people arguing with you about the merits of different singers or bands? Maddy, who was a dance music diva, thought my genre of choice was quaintly middle-aged. Out came the imaginary pipe whenever I talked about a folk album or artist.

I was queueing at the Deaf Institute bar patiently with other well-behaved folkies when a female voice behind me asked, "Have you seen them before?"

I turned to see an attractive, petite woman with long, chestnut hair and hazel eyes standing behind me. We got chatting and met for a drink after the show. I felt relaxed with her straight away and it seemed the most natural thing in the world for us to see each other the next night and the night after that and…

Relaxed had been the theme of my relationship with Liz until recently. We moved in together three months after we met. She had just started her teaching career and I was doing well as a freelance business psychologist, so we could just about afford to rent a small flat in a not-too-grim part of the city.

If you are lucky (that word again), there are times in your life when things just go well. Career, relationships, health and so on are all good. You make progress on all fronts and nothing seems too much of a slog. Our first year in the flat was one of those golden periods. We even helped each other with work stuff. As an English teacher, Liz was well placed to help me polish my presentations, both written and oral. She drew on my knowledge about learning to design her lessons and courses. Between us we made Shakespeare fascinating to her sceptical students, and at the same time the Bard stealthily infiltrated my subconscious.

They say all good things come to an end, but in my experience you don't always realise when it's happened. Little by little, my work began edging Liz into the background for me. She was dead busy too, so we carried on as if nothing had changed between us. At some level though, we both sensed there were problems, so naturally we got engaged. I felt I could relax again as Liz once more fitted effortlessly into the arc of my success story.

My 'London Idea' created the first obvious tension between Liz and me. I had applied to People People Inc through LinkedIn on a whim without even mentioning it to her. Once I'd been invited to the first on-screen interview, I told her about it, saying it would probably come to nothing. She was not amused, but as the assessment process moved through its seemingly interminable stages she seemed to come around to the idea. There was more friction when the stark reality of being apart and giving up the flat took hold. However, by the time I packed my bags for the London train I think she had got behind the plan.

Our Zoom started and after the usual pleasantries I told Liz about Julia's cryptic message. I thought with my project now on hold that she would welcome the chance to talk more often and at greater length. She was always complaining that I put work commitments before her. I'd explained all about delayed gratification and the pay-off for sacrifices in the short term. Sadly, even the promise of a glittering lifestyle to come didn't stop her sulking. Anyway, here I was with time on my hands and now she was the one with essays and papers to mark, lessons to prepare, extracurricular activities to run and suchlike, so twice-a-week calls were still the deal. I wouldn't have minded if she had shown some enthusiasm as I waxed lyrical about the newfound joys of west London, but she seemed tepid at best.

"How about you come down next weekend and I show you around Kang's Domain?" I asked.

She frowned. "I've agreed to referee the year three footy game on the Saturday," she responded.

I was about to suggest the weekend after when I realised that by then I would hopefully be back in the swing of work and if I rescinded the invite she would be really pissed off. So we left it open-ended and our call dribbled to its conclusion.

As I sat in my comfortable, well-appointed new abode, I imagined Liz scrunched up in the single bed squeezed into her childhood room. Surely a wild weekend with me in the lap of luxury should beat that? Another of Grumpus's sailing metaphors came to mind: "You can tack the boat all you like, lad, but if there's no wind, you're staying put."

Gentle, Mental Giant

Feeling rather disgruntled after my call, I switched on the TV to watch the news. I quickly wished I hadn't bothered. It was full of depressing and repetitive stuff about the flu, or 'coronavirus', apparently, which now seemed to be breaking out all over the world. I wondered if this was somehow connected to my pilot project being postponed.

The news bulletin had featured the prime minister reassuring us all that there was really nothing to worry about. This from a man who didn't appear to take anything seriously. My hard head told me that he was probably right, but I also recalled my naïve, youthful self listening to Grumpus say, "D'you know how to tell when politicians are lying, lad?"

I shook my head.

"Their lips are moving."

I went into the kitchen and poured myself a cheering glass of red wine. Kang didn't seem to have alcoholic drinks of any kind in the flat but so far had not objected to my standard couple of bottles polluting his cupboard and fridge.

I wondered if my mate Micky (The Gentle Mental Giant, as I called him behind his back) would be up for a call. He was what Grumpus called a twofer. That meant a friend who was also useful. Being a hefty physical specimen, Micky had been a handy guy to hang round with at school, but his bodyguarding services were no longer relevant to his appeal. Fortunately, he was also a mathematical brain on legs who had developed a nifty algorithm for my employee motivation system and let me have it for nothing.

I'd had the brilliant idea of enabling companies to tailor their motivation packages to each individual employee. They would get the maximum value from each one with virtually no wasted cost. Happy days. Problem was, I didn't quite know how to work this magic. About a year ago I'd mentioned my problem to Micky in passing. Despite his vast cognitive abilities my friend had given a swerve to higher education and all the career opportunities that would have been open to him. He was quite content to work in his elder brother's record shop and have ample time for his multiple and varied hobbies. Luckily for me, these included many aspects of technology. The day after I'd moaned to him about the problem of executing my bright idea, he sent me an email saying "Try this" with the algorithm attached.

I had no problem getting some willing, and free, volunteers to test out my new system. People are such suckers for thinking they will learn more about themselves. With only a few further adjustments I soon had something that actually worked. I would need access to an organisation with a large workforce and deep pockets to finance the system, but I knew that somehow I would find the right customer. The more pressing issue was how much money I would need to shell out to get exclusive rights to the all-important algorithm from its creator. I didn't want some fancy lawyer turning up in future demanding Micky's cut.

I had fully prepared myself for some hard bargaining with Micky once I'd decided that his algorithm would be a real asset. We met at his folksy local boozer, The Cemetery, over pints of murky real ale. He looked incongruous with his Rastaman hair and Bob Marley T-shirt among the pallid, tweedy, real ale enthusiasts.

"Full of twigs and bits of beak, Joe," he quipped, clinking our glasses.

"Cheers." I sipped mine and put it down, heroically managing to swallow the vile mouthful.

"Now, about **my** algorithm," I started, deliberately staking my claim. "There's the question of a fee for your contribution. To be fair, I suggest–"

I was cut off by Micky as he set down his empty glass. "It's sick that algorithm, innit?" he said. "Don't worry, bruh. Free an' gratis."

After decoding Micky's Lancashire-accented slang mash-up, I concluded that he didn't want a fee or share of any profits.

"Are you sure?" I asked, feeling disarmed by his generosity.

"Course. You'll need every cent to pay for yer fancy weddin' reception. Nuthin' but the best for you and the luvly Liz. 'Ere's lookin' at you kids!"

He'd somehow rustled up another pint, which he downed in one as a toast. I reluctantly followed suit, recalling a Grumpus lecture about gift horses and their mouths.

The main reason Micky came to my mind on that gloomy evening was that he genuinely understood stuff like exponential growth and such arcane concepts. If anybody I knew would have a sensible view about this coronavirus and its impact, Micky would be the one.

It had been a while since we'd spoken. To be honest, as his usefulness declined, I'd found his company less compelling; a semi barnacle, really. He was part of the Manchester world I'd left behind and I just assumed he would fade out of my life. Maybe he felt the same, as he'd made no great effort to stay in touch. However, it might be time to activate The Gentle Mental Giant again, so I sent him a text: "long time no talk mick fancy a catch up cheers j".

He never replied.

Last Night

For as long as I could remember I had always been a busy, busy guy. Not in a random headless chicken way but always purposefully thinking about how I could get ahead and making things happen.

"If you can fill the unforgiving minute with sixty seconds of distance run..." Grumpus used to quote from Kipling as he threw me another knotted rope, or sheet, as he claimed sailors called them, to untangle. He had certainly lived by that principle. A talented engineer and gifted entrepreneur, as he immodestly described himself, he had built a thriving business in the construction industry and sold it for a small fortune just before he turned sixty. He then promptly retired, decamped himself and Gran from cosy Stockport to the middle of nowhere, and bought himself a boat.

The boat became my grandfather's obsession. He boasted about how good a sailor you had to be to manage a 'thirty-footer' single-handedly and there was always something needed to maintain or improve it. Thus were his unforgiving minutes filled.

Grumpus made no secret of his contempt for my dad's hours spent meditating. "Sat round with his finger up his backside," as he described it. As was often the way in families, I had skipped a generation and copied my driven granddad rather than my Zen father. Mind you, my father had been a go-getter himself until his heart attack at the tender age of forty-three. He'd been travelling the world for most of my childhood before that, running various charitable programmes.

"Charity begins at home – not that my half-baked son seems to appreciate that!" Grumpus had declared.

It was disorientating not to be fully occupied with my projects and plans, and I hated it. I felt restless to the point of agitation as the weekend gaped.

I had at last received an invite from Julia's PA for my delayed meeting with the boss. It was scheduled for tomorrow morning, even though it was Saturday. No problem, as I only did weekends when I was with Liz; otherwise, it was a seven-day week for yours truly. The meeting would be on screen, not in person. This was no surprise after the government's recent warning against 'unnecessary social contact'. I wondered how long that was going to last and when I would be able to resume work on my breakthrough project.

That evening I was surprised when Kang invited me to his "FRIDAY MOVIE NIGHT!" out of the blue and was initially inclined to join him out of sheer boredom.

He ushered me into the living room, then pointed to the large screen and projector lowering electronically from the ceiling and the rear speakers that had previously been concealed behind wall panels. Two comfy armchairs facing the screen were separated by a small table for drinks and snacks. I was weakening until Kang announced, "Tonight is *Harry Potter and Half Blood Prince*. BEST BOOK AND BEST OF MOVIES!"

This was the kind of whimsical nonsense that Liz favoured. I'd had to make it clear very early in our relationship that she could count me out of anything involving wizards, elves, talking animals or, for that matter, spaceships. They were all in a category I thought of as Ridiculous Guff I Wouldn't Waste My Precious Time On. I had no intention of changing that policy now or ever.

"I'm really sorry, but I've arranged to meet up with some friends from work this evening." I hadn't, of course. The idea of my being pals with anybody at People People Inc was laughable. Ruthless competition was a core company value and chummy overtures were seen as a gambit in the unceasing game of getting ahead of your rivals.

Kang seemed to take my excuse at face value. "HAHA! Last chance to 'get one in', eh?"

His comment reminded me that this was the final day that pubs, bars, restaurants and so on would be open, courtesy of yet another government announcement.

"Oh yes," I blustered. "Can't miss the chance to 'down a few' with my mates."

Without another word, Kang ushered me into the

hall and closed the doors behind me. Soon afterwards the overblown movie theme music struck up and I heard Kang bellow, "FIFTY POINTS TO GRYFFINDOR!"

Definitely the right decision to give this entertainment a miss.

I stood in the hall and wondered why I had not just told Kang I wasn't interested in watching the movie. Fear he would chuck me out on the street? Pull yourself together, Joe!

I felt it was best to leave the flat for a couple of hours, but where to go? I put my jacket on and descended to the street. I'd already had some food, so a restaurant or café didn't appeal. Pub? Never my favourite haunt. As Grumpus put it, "Same old half-cut lot every night talking same old drivel." However, the lights in the window of KPYRO caught my eye. What the hell.

The place was heaving and the noise level probably equal to a Heathrow airstrip at take-off as the locals made the most of their last drunken revel. I somehow found a space by the bar. Giving the toxic *Lobotomiya Frontal* a miss, I ordered a pint of *Baltika* lager – 'Russia's most popular beer', as it proclaimed itself. It wasn't bad and at half the price would have been fair value.

The barman, a young Irish guy, was one of those rare individuals who could somehow navigate the swirling chaos of a crowded bar without missing a beat. Definitely a PhD subject there for some enterprising young psychologist. As my empty glass touched the bar, he was in front of me offering a refill. I rubbed my hands together and replied, "Make it a pint."

He looked at me and asked, "Will I open a tab for you?"

"Why not?" I unwisely assented.

Three drinks later, I had progressed to Scotch, and the eerie conviviality of the bar around me had reached a hysterical pitch. Guffawing lads and shrieking lasses vied for life and soul of the party status. I was feeling pretty mellow myself by this stage, when who should appear at the bar beside me, spilling my drink as they elbowed their way in, but Dumb and Dumber from my previous visit. They were even further along the road to a snooze in the gutter than on my last sighting. Certainly, their garbled nonsense was even harder to ignore this time around.

"Let down!" the hefty one bellowed. "I thought Boris was a good bloke; knows what's what, y'know. But here he is, closin' all the enter… enter… er places where you can chill. What a pussy!"

His scrawny mate friend nodded vigorously while slopping his drink on the bar, from where it dribbled slowly into his lap. "No football either!" he moaned.

The hulk wagged his finger and continued.

"Well, I'm not 'avin' it. I told the old lady my mates will be comin' round every night from now on for a few drinkies and a snort or two. She knows better than to contradict me, know what I mean?"

The second speaker concluded by slapping his hand down on the bar, which caused his spilt drink to splash up on him but also onto my sleeve. Now, I am not a guy who gets into fights or even arguments. Under verbal assault I tend to close it down and think of some ingenious and unattributable way to get back at my assailant. If things turn physical, I'm not ashamed to run away.

"Speed beats strength most of the time," Grumpus was wont to say. But that night before lockdown suddenly my blood was up.

"'Ey, saddo," I hissed. "Ave you and yer mate left t' brain cell yeh share at 'ome?" I'd definitely lapsed into an Oldham accent by this stage, aping the tough guys at my secondary school.

There was what you might call a pregnant pause. The two lushes pushed themselves away from the bar, and I swear I could hear the gears turning as they struggled to absorb what I'd said.

I guess that when sober the bigger moron could have put me down with a sharp punch to the jaw. Rat-arsed as he was tonight, his left-handed hook came in slow motion. He had also overlooked the fact that the smaller idiot was in between us, so instead of connecting with my face his fist crashed into his pal's ear.

"Owww, shit!" the man in the middle cried, and slumped

against the bar.

His fearsome friend was winding up for another go at me when the barman vaulted impressively over the counter, baseball bat in hand. I guess he didn't have a nice game of rounders in mind as he grabbed the bigger of my would-be assailants by the arm and yelled, "Youse two get out now before I call the feds. And when we open up again yer barred, FOREVER!"

It took a few minutes for the grumbling miscreants to stagger out of the bar's front door. My rescuer watched them all the way before turning to me and saying with a grin, "I heard what you said to those dickheads. Couldn't have put it better myself!"

He offered me a drink on the house, but I declined with thanks, saying I'd had enough.

When I tried to settle my bill, he waved away my credit card and said in a cod American gangster accent, "Yer money's no good here, buddy. Tanks for de cabaret." Then he continued, "I'm Conor Nolan, by the way, manager of this hostelry. Assuming we ever open again, your next drink is on the house too."

I introduced myself and said I hoped to take him up on his kind offer. He turned to a pretty young blonde woman behind the bar who was taking a quick breather from the melee in front of it and called her over. She smiled as she approached us, her stormy blue eyes flashing as if she was actually looking forward to meeting me.

"This is my smarter twin sister, Chloe," he explained. "She's taking time out from her studies, at the London School of Economics; Master's in Business and Management no less, to help her poor brother out. Chloe, meet my new mate Joe, who kindly gave me an excuse to bar your two least favourite customers."

"Ah, no more visits from the gorilla and the weasel! Thanks for that, Joe," she said with a glorious smile. "What's your family name?"

This was a bit unexpected, but I stuttered, "D-d-dunne."

"Now, Joseph Dunne, that smacks of Irish heritage. Am I right?"

I recalled Grumpus's advice never to look back. "Where you're going is what matters! Where you or your family comes from doesn't mean a fig." My dad never seemed too bothered about his Dunne genealogy either.

"No idea, I'm afraid," I replied.

Undeterred, Chloe came back with, "Get yourself over here when the lockdown's finished, Joe, and we'll uncover your Oirish ancestry. Right, back to the grind," she concluded, turning toward her now clamoring customers.

"Our Chloe is a terrible flirt, Joe," warned Conor with a grin as I turned to the exit. He redirected me out of the building's rear entrance. "You don't want to have round two if your sparring partners have sobered up and are waiting at the front door. See you whenever."

My mind was on pretty Chloe as I threaded my way through the drunken throng now spread to all sides of the building. However, another fragment of my grandfather's wisdom broke through. "Affairs are for wasters. Eyes on the prize and remember: happy wife, happy life."

The street outside the bar was almost as packed as the interior and the noise level nearly as high. It felt like the last party before the end of the world as sporadic singing and dancing broke out. No sign of the Chuckle Brothers, so I walked briskly to the cinema corner, staying watchful as I went. My heart was pounding when I closed the door to the street behind me. As I climbed the stairs to the apartment it felt as if the world really was ending.

Dismissal

The first day of lockdown, I woke up late with a slight hangover from the previous evening's unaccustomed indulgence. I'd also somehow managed to unset the wake-up alarm on my phone. This had caused an unplanned lie-in. Suddenly remembering my call with Julia, I leapt out of bed, then quickly showered, shaved and dressed. What was I thinking of? Drinking too much and not getting an early night before an important meeting! I grabbed some toast and coffee in the empty kitchen. Kang was nowhere to be seen. What the hell did he do all day in his out-of-bounds apartment acreage?

My meeting with Julia was scheduled for eleven. I had already thought through what I wanted to achieve from it; chiefly some clarity about what to focus on during the unknown number of lockdown weeks ahead. I had plenty of ideas and options tucked away for any turn the conversation might take.

Like all the employees in People People Inc's UK business, I notionally reported directly to Julia. No middle management deadwood in our funky, tech-driven flat organisation, folks! Paradoxically, this meant that Julia could avoid having much contact with anybody unless it suited her. I reckoned that so far in my brief career with the company I'd done a decent job at staying in her line of sight. She was a straightforward character. By no means a people person, she was quite consistent in her one-sided and transactional "don't give me that relationship crap, what can you do for me?" way. She seemed to see the commercial potential in what I was developing and that gave me a basis for influencing her. I just had to keep her onside until the pilot project showed how much money it could make. Then she'd be wanting time in **my** calendar!

I went for a brisk walk down to the park to clear my head. The weather had turned incongruously sunny and warm as we all entered the unknown and threatening realm of lockdown. The Park and the streets around it were almost deserted. The few people I saw looked slightly furtive, as if they were breaking curfew. Some were wearing medical face masks although the government had claimed they were useless. As I crossed it, even the mighty Fulham Road, usually thrumming with morning traffic, was relatively quiet. In the window of the deserted cinema, fear still ate the soul.

Once I was settled in my room, I did some visualising and breathing exercises in preparation for the call. Meeting by video was the norm in People People Inc, as the entire business had grown on the back of increased remote working. Despite this, Julia was notorious for joining them late or not at all, so I was surprised when I was instantly connected with her instead of lingering in the virtual waiting room.

She was obviously working from home with its

meticulously arranged background: Lulu Lytle decor (or so I had been informed), expensive-looking abstract art works and image-enhancing book selection in her boho chic bookcase. The revered leader herself wore a characteristic outfit pitched somewhere between a weekend in the Hamptons and a due diligence meeting in Silicon Valley; a look few could pull off. Her jacket was immaculately tailored but in a pale blue linen that looked perfect for a poolside lunch. Beneath that her plain ivory top shimmered in the way only the most expensive silk did. Her feature necklace of slightly rustic blue gemstones provided the finishing touch.

Maddy, who was always eager to discuss high-end clothes and accessories, loved the sound of this item when I was describing my boss to her and said of it, "Sounds like a Devon Leigh Denim Lapis Cluster, Joe. You're talking about a few thousand bucks there. You couldn't take a picture of her, could you?" I declined the opportunity to risk my career in satisfying my friend's couture curiosity.

Most of my new colleagues, certainly the newbies like me, were in awe of Julia. Her cut-glass, posh accent and air of superiority had them bowing and scraping. Not wanting to be too deferential myself I had made up my own back story for her as Mavis from Luton, putting on airs and graces but ever anxious that her humble origins would be revealed. This thought was in my mind as we started our call.

My boss and I exchanged brief greetings and I waited for Julia to give me some idea of what the meeting was for. I expected an update about the pilot study and an indication of what I should focus on in the short term. Maybe I would be put on furlough, a scheme just announced by the government? However, this was Julia's meeting. She wasted no time getting to the point.

"I'll get straight to it, Joe; we have decided to let you go." She paused briefly to let that sink in. "This pandemic will create unprecedented opportunities for our core products, so we don't anticipate any need for your 2.0 model in the foreseeable future."

I started to object, emphasising the masses of evidence showing that my approach was far more likely to increase productivity than the basic carrot and stick. Maybe I could go on furlough until the situation became a bit more normal?

She cut me off. "Y'know, I really couldn't give a shit about the statistics. If clients believe something works and want to buy some more that's good enough for me. From now on, **everyone** will be working from home, and companies will be paranoid as hell about what their employees are up to. No need for any of that kumbaya bullshit of yours. They have less than zero interest in coaching, developing, motivating and all those other 'ings' you want to sell them. All they want to do is spy on their employees and fire them if they think they're lazy. I think the tide will be running in that direction for quite some time to come thanks to our buddy Mister Covid."

I tried desperately to keep the conversation going on the basis that if I was still talking there was a chance of influencing the outcome.

"I'm sure I can adapt and contribute to the core business.

I've got some ideas already that I can lay out for you!"

Julia stared at me with an unnerving expression, known in the company as her 'Kubrick Stare', like the one Jack Nicholson's character in *The Shining* had. Never having seen the movie, I had streamed it to get an idea of what my colleagues were on about. After half an hour of Nicholson's one-note performance, I understood. I had also created a new category, exclusively for horror films: Ridiculous And Nasty Guff I Wouldn't Waste My Precious Time On.

Julia's tone was distinctly chilly as she said, "You know, you rather had me fooled when you first joined us, Joe, but you're not what you seem. To make it in my world what you see has to be what you get: with you, what I've seen is a shell, and sooner or later I think it would crack. You think you're a predator but you're not. Maybe you aren't prey, either, but I doubt that what's in between is much use to me. Anyway, Human Ops will be in touch with you about your severance terms. And by the way, don't forget that if you approach any of our clients our lawyers will 'crush you like a bug', as Luke puts it."

Before I could react, Julia administered her coup de grace. Plastering one of her classic insincere smiles on her face she said, "Oh, and don't worry about the pilot scheme. Once everyone has settled into a pandemic working mode, Chuck will be managing the client's transition to our 'original, and best' Performance Tracking system."

Then she terminated the meeting without so much as a goodbye, good luck, or thanks for trying.

I sat staring in shock at the Zoom home screen for a full twenty minutes. I knew a lot (or so I thought) about how people responded to change: shock, denial, anger, blame, depression and eventually problem-solving and so on. This was no consolation whatever as I contemplated the implosion of my meticulously planned destiny.

When my confusion had subsided a bit, I briefly considered sending Julia the recording I had made of Chuck, slagging her off. I even began preparing to send the clip to her, but another bit of Grumpus lore stayed my finger. His view of revenge was; if someone gets the better of you and you have a chance for vengeance then take it if, and only if, it also puts you in a better position.

"But what about if you just want the satisfaction of paying them back?" I had challenged.

Grumpus gave me one of his pitying looks. "Waste of time. Just get over it and move on." He paused for effect. "And if you do retaliate, make sure it works and don't leave any fingerprints!"

As I closed my system, I had a fleeting memory of once helping Liz to prepare a lesson about revenge in *Macbeth*. One of the lines was: "Let grief convert to anger; blunt not the heart, enrage it."

Yeah, how did that work out for you, Mac?

I went and made myself a coffee just for something to

do. I looked around the luxurious kitchen and felt a pang of anticipatory loss. Just when I'd landed in this fabulous place to live, my income stream had run dry. Well, screw that. I was Joe Dunne, the man with a plan. One door closed? I'd kick open another one!

By Sunday morning I had formulated my Plan B. I was confident it would give me an even faster path to success than the People People Inc route. London was still the right place for me, but no more relying on a conventional organisation for my platform. Networks were the way of the future. I regarded most social media as mere barnacle accumulators but I was a LinkedIn Ninja. I would use lockdown to get my most useful contacts aligned, ready to hit the road running when things went back to normal.

I could see now that People People Inc wasn't a mistake as such. It had been the catalyst I needed to steer myself away from shallow waters and moderate breezes into the strong currents and wild gusts where I would thrive. Blow winds and crack your cheeks!

My only challenge was how to cover my living expenses once my last pay from the consultant job was gone, which wouldn't take long. Hopefully in a couple of months I'd get some initial income flowing from freelance work, but that gap had to be bridged.

Fortunately, Liz and I had been saving toward our wedding, honeymoon and even the deposit for our own flat. There wasn't a fortune in the account, but just about enough to keep going if we pushed the wedding plans back to next year. I sent Liz a message straight away suggesting a call that evening.

I was feeling pretty pumped about my new business ideas, so even Liz's reply saying "Tomorrow 7PM?" didn't irritate me as much as it otherwise might have. I was bursting to share my enthusiasm with someone, though, so I called Maddy as she would be back in the UK by now. No possibility of meeting in person due to the new Covid rules, but there was plenty to catch up on.

Frustratingly, Maddy's number went straight to voicemail. "Hi. You've reached Maddy. Well, nearly! Leave a message, keep it short and hope I ring you back. Bye!"

I left my message demanding she return my call ASAP and continued to sit in the kitchen drumming my fingers on the table.

I hadn't noticed that Kang was now also in the kitchen, making himself his usual giant espresso, a kind of double doppio. Wow, he must get wired after one of those. As usual he ignored me, but I looked at him attentively and noticed that he seemed not to be his normal bustling self. His face was rather drawn, and did his shoulders seem slumped?

"How are you doing?" I asked.

He turned and paused before replying. "Kang has been better," he said, slowly before slouching back to his quarters.

I shrugged and began planning my new influencing

strategy. Over the years I had accumulated a healthy list of contacts despite my anti-barnacle mindset. They now required some sifting for the post People People Inc era. The great imponderable was how lockdown would affect each individual. No point wasting time cultivating somebody who was likely to be made redundant.

Sorrows Come

Monday morning and a fresh start. The weather seemed to endorse me with dazzling sunshine over west London. It was warm too, and I wished I had brought some summer clothes down with me. Nonetheless, I put on my smart casual office outfit in case I succeeded in getting an on-screen meeting with anybody during the day. I warmed up by calling a couple of contacts who were way down my list, leaving a voicemail for one and getting straight through to the other. He was predictably useless, banging on about the insecurity of his own position, so I kept the call as short as decently possible. It served its purpose, though. I was back into Joe Dunne business development mode and ready to hunt down the big game.

Before I could continue my prospecting, I received an incoming call. It was a landline number I didn't recognise so I opened with a neutral, "Hello."

"Good morning, Joe," responded a vaguely familiar voice. "This is Raj, Madhura's father."

"Oh, er, hi," I replied inanely at this unexpected turn of events.

"Joe, I just picked up your message on Madhura's phone. I'm afraid that she is very ill with Covid. She has been taken into hospital and is on a ventilator. We aren't even allowed to see her."

His voice now had a desperate tone and I began to panic. Irrelevant questions clamoured to be asked: How is she? (Answered, idiot!) Will she be okay? (Do you think anybody knows?) Which hospital is she in? (Planning to rush over and break her out or what?) Is there anything I can do? (Best of a bad bunch, if useless.)

"Oh, Raj, I'm so sorry. Is there anything I can do to help?"

"Thank you for offering, Joe, but I think that all any of us can do is wait and pray. The people at the hospital say they will call us about any change in her condition. I promise I will let you know any news."

Given Maddy's extended family, I realised I would be well down the list to contact, but I thanked him gratefully and sent all my best wishes to the family, especially Maddy.

As I put the phone down, I felt as if I had been kicked in the stomach. The People People Inc bombshell had been bad enough, but this shook me to my core. Not Maddy. She was young and super fit and…she was my indefatigable Maddy! I was also startled to realise that Maddy was my best friend. Even more than Liz (in fact, much more than Liz), she was the one I could tell anything to and not be judged or played. In the absence of anybody to pray to I sat and hoped that she would be okay.

I couldn't bring myself to make any more calls that afternoon. (Hi, it's Joe here. My best friend might be dying. How are you?) I took a brief walk in the spring sunshine but was too freaked out by the post-apocalyptic-style silent streets to make it to the park. Nowhere open, of course, and the few people I saw rushed past me, heads down as if even eye contact could spread the plague.

As I rounded my home corner, the *Fear Eats The Soul* posters in the cinema window caught my eye. I'd only ever glanced at them before, assuming the film was some tedious horror gorefest. I looked more closely at the main image of a slightly weird-looking man and woman locked in a tender yet somehow desperate embrace. They didn't seem happy. I resolved to stream a James Bond movie after my call with Liz. Maybe I could persuade her to watch it simultaneously as we wouldn't be going out to the movies together any time soon. Who says I'm not a romantic?

Depressed further by my brief outing I went and sat in the living room just for a change of scene. Kang must have heard me because he appeared in the doorway. He looked terrible, as if he hadn't slept for days. He certainly hadn't shaved recently. I found myself wondering if he was coming down with Covid and asked if he felt okay.

"Just little tired," he replied slowly. "Working very hard at moment."

I still had no idea what his work consisted of, so I took his word for that.

His voice sounded wearier than ever when, with no preamble, he explained that he would be receiving a delivery during the night. Then he walked over to my seat and loomed over me, continuing, "VERY PRIVATE! If you wake you must stay in bedroom!"

This was more like the peremptory Kang I had become used to. I knew better than to ask for any details so I just reassured him that a) I was famous for sleeping like the dead and b) If I did wake, I would stay under the sheets.

This seemed to satisfy him, and he turned away looking slumped and tired again.

In more normal circumstances I would probably have focused on Kang and his midnight delivery and wondered what the hell was going on. As it was, I was preoccupied with more pressing stuff, so I pretty much forgot about it.

Chickens Roosting

I wasn't particularly looking forward to my call with Liz. Two pieces of really bad news to share and a suggestion about finances that she would hardly welcome. She hadn't even seemed that thrilled about my recent good news, so this conversation would take careful handling. Plenty of "how was your day, are you getting on with your folks" questions and some serious effort to look interested required up front.

I opened the call screen a few minutes ahead of the start time as usual. Confronted by myself, I wished I hadn't changed into T-shirt and jeans as this wasn't going to be the usual small talk call. I wondered if I had time to change back into something smarter, but Liz was characteristically punctual in joining the call.

As we exchanged our usual pleasantries, I noticed unusual things about on-screen Liz. For a start, she was distinctly closer to her camera than normal, revealing less of her bedroom background. The small area that I could see looked different yet still strangely familiar.

"Liz," I interrupted whatever she'd been saying, "where

are you?"

She blushed and cast her eyes down as she hesitantly replied. "Er, Joe, this is very difficult, and I didn't want to rush into telling you, but… I've been very lonely since you moved to London. It's been really hard being back at home."

I'd heard all this before but put on my sympathetic listening face.

"I've been spending time with Micky, and he's been a real friend in need."

"Hang on a second," I interrupted again. "Gentle Mental Giant Micky? You've never mentioned this before!"

"Joe," she pressed on, "Micky and I have become more than friends recently, and he invited me to stay with him when lockdown started."

Liz had gradually moved back from her camera as we spoke. Over her left shoulder, I now saw the telltale corner of Micky's Burning Spear poster.

"You're telling me you've moved in with Micky? **Micky**? What about us?"

She seemed flustered, but her face changed and she looked directly back at me out of the screen.

"There is no 'us', Joe, is there? There's you, you, you, and me as an afterthought. It's been like that ever since you came up with this London idea. Maybe it's always been like that. I don't know, Joe."

I sat looking at Liz on the screen, not knowing what to say.

She broke the silence. "Joe. I'm sorry if this hurts you, though I don't even know if it does; whether you even care that much. I know there's a few things to sort out: wedding money and that sort of stuff. I'll drop you an email about it."

I thought she was going to end on this mundane note, but her face changed again and she looked sad as she said, "This is probably a ridiculous thing to say, but I hope that somehow we can be friends in the future. You can be a smashing bloke. And I don't believe that what you think you want is what you really need."

She had started to cry and hurriedly said goodbye, then left the call.

Night Delivery

I spent the rest of that day in a daze, not even remembering to eat. I briefly had the news on in my room, but it was dominated by the pandemic. That made me think of Maddy perhaps fighting for her life in hospital.

Lying on the bed and staring at the ceiling, I began to wonder if luck had somehow turned against me. Grumpus would have chided me for such weak-willed musing, but I felt as if the tide of my fortunes was ebbing away from me too quickly for me to catch it.

I turned the TV off and put in my EarPods so I could listen to some music. Liz and I went to a lot of gigs when we first got together. One of our favourites was the annual Christmas gig by Kate Rusby at various venues around the northwest. I went to the relevant playlist to put me in mind of happier times. It just made me much sadder. Then a non-festive tune of Kate's started up, 'Underneath The Stars'. Liz loved this song and always cried at:

"Underneath the stars you met me
And there beneath the stars you left me

I wonder if the stars regret me
I'm sure they'd like me if they only met me
They come and go of their own free will
Go gently"

I started crying and then couldn't stop. I heard Grumpus's voice in my mind saying, "Weepin's for kiddies. Real men never blub."

Bugger off, Grumpus…

I woke up and realised that I had fallen asleep with my Pods in. I took them out and massaged my numb ears. I looked down at my crumpled clothes and groaned. My phone showed the unearthly hour of 03.33. I knew I should get up, clean my teeth, get undressed and properly go to bed. Instead, I lay on my back trying not to think of anything.

After about half an hour in a trance, more mindless than mindful, my stupor was interrupted by the sound of the front door closing. I instantly remembered Kang's mysterious delivery, went to the window and, disobeying orders, opened the blinds slightly. I caught a brief glimpse of a van disappearing down the street. Then I heard a sound on the stairs. It was a muted thump, thump, which I concluded was something heavy being brought up them. Occasionally there was a groan as (presumably) Kang laboured with the burden.

There was silence for a minute or two, then the door to the flat opened quietly. I thought I could hear the sound of wheels like those on a suitcase trundling along the hall. I considered opening my door to see what was going on, but this was not the moment to piss off Kang and become homeless. In any event, I heard the door to his room open and close and then no more sounds.

Despite a rush of adrenaline due to the nocturnal disturbance, I now felt incredibly tired. I quickly got ready for bed at last and slid gratefully under the duvet. I put a mental dam in place to hold back the flood of thoughts and feelings that threatened to overwhelm me and fell into a dreamless sleep.

The Call

The next day also started later than I was used to. I am definitely a morning person and like to be up and at 'em while others are still rubbing their eyes. On this occasion it was after ten o'clock by the time I slumped into the kitchen for some breakfast. I had barely started tucking into my muesli when I was joined by Kang.

This morning he was sporting jeans and a bright red sweatshirt whose brand logo suggested it cost more than my parents' car. He still looked a bit frayed around the edges but was full of his old vigour as he uncharacteristically bade me a hearty "GOOD MORNING!"

I responded with as much cheer as I could muster as he picked out one of the mud-coloured drinks he kept in the fridge. I'd seen him making these in a blender out of various unfamiliar fruits and vegetables. The resulting liquid smelt like the exotic plants greenhouse in Wythenshawe Park, near where I'd lived as a kid. It was earthy, rich and possibly not for human consumption. He didn't need to worry about me swiping one of those.

My host was clearly a healthy eater and (non) drinker. He also looked fit and lean, but as I'd never seen him leave the flat I wondered how he managed to stay so toned. Moonlight Tai Chi sessions in Battersea Park, perhaps?

"It is going to be OUTSTANDING DAY!" Kang announced, clapping me on the back on his way out. I nearly choked on my cereal and wondered just what last night's consignment had been.

"Don't get high on your own supply," I muttered after him.

Liz's shock announcement had left me with plenty to think about. I pushed away thoughts that in some way it was my fault that our relationship had crashed and burned. Easier to wallow in resentment for now. One pressing issue was money. My plan to hit the wedding fund while I created a new income stream down in London now looked shaky. It wasn't a huge amount to begin with, but half of it wouldn't go that far. I wasn't giving up on my dreams just yet, but the harsh reality was that I needed a back-up in case the pandemic turned out to be more serious than we'd all been told. Time to contact my folks.

I guess that many people's childhoods follow a gradual trajectory where circumstances, relationships and other fundamentals are established early, and those patterns are by and large followed. But for some there is a disruption that changes everything. In my case, it was THE CALL.

We lived in leafy Didsbury when I was a kid, in a

comfortable semi with a decently sized, well-tended garden. Mam was ahead of her time, working as a physiotherapist at home in a converted bedroom. Dad was a senior programme manager in an international charity. He was away a lot, doing good around the world and coming home tired and wanting his own space for a bit. Eventually, though, he would always relent and tell me about the exotic places he had visited and the people he had met. Overall, I was lucky; Mam provided security and continuity while I dreamed of Dad's adventures and made the most of his time at home.

THE CALL came when I was eleven. Mam was in the kitchen, so I answered the phone. The line was crackly, but I could make out a man's voice that I didn't recognise asking to speak to Helen Dunne. "It concerns her husband, Daniel. It is very urgent!" the stranger emphasised.

I called Mam and handed her the receiver then turned away. Like most kids, I had little interest in grown-ups' conversations, but some instinct made me sit down on the sofa and listen to Mam's side of the call. By the time it finished I knew that the news was bad. When Mam put the phone down and explained what the man had said, I realised it was terrible.

Dad had had a heart attack while travelling between meetings in Zimbabwe. He had been rushed to hospital for surgery, which had been successful, and was now under observation until he had recovered sufficiently to return to the UK.

Young as I was, I could tell that Mam was editing her account to reassure me. I spent the period until Dad returned home in a state of panic, convinced he was never coming back.

In a sense, the dad I had known never returned from Africa. His dynamic, even adventurous, character turned quieter, more cautious and reflective. He was strongly advised that a less stressful lifestyle was essential for his health, and he took that counsel seriously. Abandoning his globetrotting charities career, he morphed into a one-man local repair shop. He had always been a wiz at mending things around the house on the occasions he was home, and now he fixed the knackered equipment of the neighbourhood's more frugal or conservation-minded citizens. This not-too-taxing occupation served to pay the bills, just about, but we couldn't afford to stay in Didsbury; we were moving to Oldham.

I was exiled from my dreamy, gentle suburban life to the harsh realities of a down-at-heel Lancashire town. Our new house was in one of many anonymous, sprawling developments. It was cramped compared to the old one and had a postage-stamp garden. However, the neighbours were pretty welcoming, and my mother could get along with anyone. Dad's years of mingling with all sorts of people around the world stood him in good stead too. That just left me.

Plans to attend a well-regarded local college in Didsbury along with kids I knew from primary school had to be abandoned. In September 2004, I found myself trudging the grimy corridors of Blackstone School, an establishment with a spotty reputation at best. It was the only school with a place available for me at short notice. I couldn't imagine anyone battling to get into Blackstone, though I could readily understand them fighting to escape it.

I didn't know a single person. All the other pupils were local, and many knew each other. In the first lesson we were told to introduce ourselves to the class. I said as little as possible but in what I thought was an I'm-just-a-regular-lad way. Nevertheless, among the blank, bored expressions, I saw a few that were overtly hostile. I guessed they wouldn't be rolling out the red carpet for a newcomer with a non-Oldham accent.

It didn't take long for my fears to be realised. Four hard-looking lads confronted me in the playground at the morning break. One of them stabbed his finger in my chest. "Oo d'ye think you are, posh boy?" he spat. "Think you're better than us do you, pouf?"

I considered whether "moronic bigot" or "bigoted moron" would work better as a response, guessing either would earn me a good kicking. Then a huge, dreadlocked lad pushed through the others and held an immense fist out to me. It took a moment for me to realise that this was for bumping rather than punching, so I took his cue.

In a deep but surprisingly soft voice, he said, "'Iya, bruh. Welcome to Blackstone. Ah'm Micky, from the second year, eh?" He then turned to my antagonists and said, "Orright, lads?"

They nodded vigorously and quickly vanished. I was about to thank my rescuer for his help when he turned to me and said quietly, "You'll need to try and fit in, mate. Know worra mean?"

Taking Micky's advice to heart, I did my best not to antagonise the kids in school or outside. In a strange way, it was probably the start of my interest in psychology. For example, it always amazed me that while I never heard Micky threaten, let alone hit anyone or even raise his voice, all the other lads deferred to him. Through my own efforts and my association with my hulking mate, any bullying I experienced was minimal, even after Micky left school the year before I did. The rejection though, was constant. I blamed my father for it all.

Bequest

Looking back as an adult, I suspected there was some financial element involved, because from my first school holiday after we'd moved to Oldham at every break I was packed off for a week, or more in summer, to stay with my grandfather.

I was glad to get away and to be outdoors most of the time. At first, my grandfather's bluntness and strong opinions were hard to take. I had been raised to try and see both sides of an argument, but with Grumpus it was his way or sling yer 'ook. Over the next few years, I came to embrace his black-and-white view of the world. "Enlightened self-interest," he called it, and that simple philosophy became my shield against a world grown suddenly harsh.

My dad and his father had never seen eye to eye. Gran had died when I was four and I had no real memory of her, but Dad had clearly been fond of his mum and in the few photos she appeared in, her twinkling smile contrasted with her husband's typical scowl. After her death, the old man continued to live by himself in the rambling family home on the Fylde coast, spending more time on his beloved boat than in the house. Apart from my regular working holidays in Fylde

I had no contact with him. I must admit that I pretty much lost touch after going to university, and Grumpus wasn't exactly the Christmas card type.

It was toward the end of my second year studying Business Psychology at Manchester that Grumpus made his last intervention in our lives, albeit from beyond the grave. We found out that he had died when out of the blue Dad and I each received a solicitor's letter inviting us to the reading of his will. We trooped off with Mam all the way up to Fleetwood so that the lawyer could run through the terms of our bequests. Grumpus clearly intended to linger in death with the same impact he'd had in life. The bulk of his quite large estate went to the Royal National Lifeboat Institute.

"I know that my son places the needy well above his own family," was the accompanying comment read out by the embarrassed-looking executor.

The solicitor explained that the bequests in relation to Dad and me were linked and had "rather unusual and complex" terms. Mam and I caught each other's eyes as Dad stared out of the window, sighing. Grumpus had put his house into a trust. I would inherit it provided Mam and Dad went to live there. It would revert to me when both had passed away. Unless they occupied the house, starting in three months' time, it would be sold and the proceeds donated to the lucky old RNLI.

Thus had the old man extended his influence on his family for years to come. We could of course have simply ignored the proffered opportunity and let the seafaring community benefit. However, after much hand wringing and soul searching, my parents sold the Oldham house and sank most of their small amount of equity into the many repairs required by the sorely neglected coastal pile.

To my relief, they still managed to apportion some money to allow me to live in Manchester for the final year of my course, as commuting from Fylde would be a challenge. As my late grandfather might have said, nautically, it's an ill wind that blows no good.

The Fylde house was located directly on the coast in a very remote location. It was gorgeous in the summer and but for my strained relationship with Dad I might have been a more regular visitor after my folks took up residence. I had no regrets giving it a miss between November and March though, when the winds lashed, and the garden was sometimes inundated by the waves. Needless to say, it had zero mobile signal and broadband of any kind could only be accessed by driving ten miles to the nearest sizeable village. Thus, I dialed their trusty old landline number to explore my new Plan B arrangements. As a last resort I might have to move back home and relaunch my business from a Fleetwood café.

I had been hoping that Mam would answer the phone but inevitably it was Dad. After a couple of awkward minutes discussing the pandemic and avoiding anything personal, I could hear the relief in his voice as he said that Mam was waiting impatiently to talk to me. The absence of hands free on their phone was a godsend. I didn't want to broach the actual subject of my coming home, nor step onto the emotional minefield of People People Inc, Liz or even Maddy. Instead, I did some indirect exploring of the main topic: were they able to see any of Mam's family and so on?

I ran into a brick wall almost immediately when Mam revealed that she and Dad were having to 'shield' as he was considered vulnerable. It was unknown when they could even receive visitors but it sounded unlikely to be any time soon. Feeling thwarted, I couldn't wait to get off the phone.

As I tried to wind it down Mam suddenly said, "Are you alright, son?" She only called me 'son' when she was worried about me, so I reassured her I was fine but concerned about them. I received assurances in return, hung up and let my head sink onto my cradled arms.

Revelation

I've always prided myself on making my time count for something. Never been a big fan of holidays and usually spent large portions of them on my laptop or phone progressing some bit of work. Whenever I'd had a setback, I focused and redoubled my efforts so I could get back on track. I couldn't stand it when people fretted and moaned instead of doing something about their situation. Thus, it really pissed me off when I realised that, after my phone call, I'd frittered away the whole day dwelling on my recent misfortunes and worrying about the future. My list of contacts sat reproachfully on the desktop reminding me of what I should have been doing as I closed down my system, resolving to have an early night and get my act together properly in the morning.

Once again it took a long time for me to fall asleep. As I tossed and turned, I began to imagine that somehow the pandemic was eating away at the foundations of my life. I knew how preposterous this was, yet the thought kept nagging away at me. What if the whole edifice I'd created for myself was about to collapse? I tried to imagine Grumpus saying "Don't be so nesh!" when I'd balk at going out to the boat on a freezing winter's day, but his mocking voice in my head was strangely silent.

In the end fatigue did its job and sleep crept up on me.

At first, I thought I was dreaming when I heard the alarm. It was a penetrating whine; not especially loud but impossible to ignore. Once awake I shot out of bed and pulled on a pair of trackies. As I went into the hall, I vaguely recalled Kang telling me about the flat's security and safety systems when I moved in and wished I'd paid more attention.

The sound was coming from his room, so I tapped, then knocked at the closed door. When this elicited no response, I bellowed "KANG!" at a level the man himself would have used. Still no reaction.

Having been repeatedly warned off Kang's quarters it felt wrong to try the door handle, but I pressed on and was admitted to a room only slightly larger than my own. The decor and furniture were similar too. On his desk the giant laptop stood open and on. Its screensaver showed a smiling young Asian woman standing on a sunlit beach and holding a large, long-haired cat in her arms.

Curiosity about my host gave way to anxiety as the alarm reminded me why I was in his room. It appeared to emanate from behind the wall facing the road side of the flat. The wall was blank but mostly covered by a hanging that depicted a dull pastoral scene. I tried lifting it and was shocked when it began to rise silently into some invisible ceiling cavity. The wall was now revealed to include a large, shut door above which a small red light flashed. There was no handle or feature of any kind on the door. I tried pushing it, but it was firmly locked or wedged. More fruitless hammering and shouting by me followed to no avail.

Being woken suddenly in the middle of the night was not conducive to clear thinking. That explained why I found myself first scrabbling to get a fingernail between door and frame and second bellowing "Open sesame!" at the top of my voice like a demented pantomime Aladdin.

Okay, let's not lose our minds here, I cautioned myself. I stood back and looked carefully at the door and the wall around it. This saner approach produced swift results. To the right of the door, at my chest height, was the faint outline of an open hand. My relief at having figured out how the door would probably open was followed by another wave of despair. The palm it needed would be attached to Kang.

But what the hell? I pressed my right palm against the print on the wall. Instantly a female voice with a distinct American accent said, "Palm not recognised!" in a vaguely challenging tone.

Shit! I started to turn away, but my brain fog must have been clearing as I suddenly remembered Kang was left-handed. So why was the palm outline on the right? I wondered. I looked at the lines again, and sure enough, illogically it was the shape of a left hand. Although I expected to be told off by the electronic voice again, I applied my left hand and, to my surprise was rewarded with "Alternate palm recognised. Door opening." If I hadn't already been so freaked out, I might have stopped to question why my 'alternate palm' had been recognised...

The door silently slid open and disappeared into its frame. The room beyond was surprisingly big and looked like some sort of high-tech lab. The lights were on, very bright but not dazzling. I could see screens, cupboards, complicated-looking bits of equipment, but not Kang. Maybe he had gone out for a late-night constitutional and would return shortly, find that I had breached his secret lab and throw me out on the street.

I dithered on the threshold and considered going back to my room, but some instinct told me I needed to go on. I stepped into the lab and the door slid shut behind me.

"Containment reestablished," the nice lady reassured me.

Containment of what? I wondered.

Most of the room was visible from where I stood. Only an area behind a sort of island in the middle was partly hidden behind a large fish tank sitting empty on its top. I peeked behind it. What looked like a large dirty pink rug was rucked up on the floor. It was incongruous against the gleaming glass and metal surfaces and the clean-enough-to-eat-off tiled floor.

Maybe it was Kang's lucky rug from home, I thought, as another bubble of hysteria floated through my confused and frightened mind.

My gaze had drifted to other objects when, from the corner of my eye, I thought I saw the rug move. I actually felt my fight or flight response kick in. My heart was pounding, my breathing was rapid and every muscle was like a bow string. My senses became hyper alert, and when I looked directly at the 'rug' I could detect slight movement as if it were rippling. I could also see that the surface was in fact lots of little spheres about the size of table tennis balls. They were grey but covered in small red growths that produced the off-pink effect. A faint glimmer of familiarity was quickly overcome by horror and revulsion, and I lurched back from the unnerving sight.

The only sound in the lab room was a faint humming of equipment, so the low groan from the ping-pong-ball rug made me jump. It was accompanied by some new movement in the grisly carpet. The central part rose slowly, creating a slight dome effect. There was another, slightly louder, groan. The dreadful possibility struck me that there might be a person (Kang?) under the spheres. My self-preservation impulse told me to turn around and run, but instead I reached forward and began frantically scraping the loathsome creatures off the figure beneath. Their growths felt slightly viscous, and my flesh crawled at their touch.

It didn't take long to find that there was indeed someone at the bottom of the pile. As more was revealed I could tell it was Kang. He struggled for breath as he got to his knees. I got my hand under his arm, and he managed to stagger to his feet. The spheres were doing their best to cling to him and several had even attached themselves to me. Fortunately, any that dropped to the floor just lay there.

Kang grabbed me and pulled me into a clear floor space where we could brush ourselves and each other clear. He was wearing a lab coat, which he discarded with its passengers still clinging on. As it hit the floor, I could see that some had crawled into the pockets.

"We must get out but make sure none of them come with us!" he gasped.

We moved to a new part of the floor and exhaustively checked for any residual infestation. Then Kang swayed to the door and hit the palm reader.

"Primary user recognised. Door opening," the disembodied voice commented.

When we were both clear, the door slid shut.

"Containment reestablished," it concluded.

I steered a stumbling Kang onto the bed, where he lay exhausted. He pointed to a cupboard and mouthed "Oxygen."

Inside there was a large cylinder thus labelled, and a dangling mask. Fitting it onto Kang's face and turning on the flow were thankfully intuitive.

I sat on the bed and watched as his breathing became more regular. My life was becoming more surreal by the moment.

Aftermath

Kang turned over and faced me. He was breathing more naturally now but looked hollow-eyed with shock. I noticed tiny marks on his face and hands, presumably from the things that had covered him. My own hands had some too; gross.

"We need to get them into the tank," he announced. "They are behaving in unexpected ways, which means unknown risks."

He began to try and sit up but immediately fell back.

"Whoah!" I cautioned. "You're in no condition to go corralling strange life forms. What the hell are they anyway?"

He looked at me intently. "Complicated to explain. Please, they must be secured in the tank. That's what I was doing when..."

"When they swarmed and nearly killed you?" I ventured.

I've seen a few people look desperate in my time, but poor Kang looked absolutely distraught. He started trying to rise again, so I put my hand on his shoulder and pushed him back down.

"You're going to stay put and recover. I'll put the little bastards to bed! Just tell me what I need to do."

As the lab door shut behind me, I briefly wondered why the hell I was putting myself at 'unknown risk'. I had no answer, so I shrugged and pressed on. Beside the doorway and under a flap was a control pad. Following Kang's instructions, I punched in a code that stopped the whining alarm. I felt less freaked out once the noise stopped.

The spheres lay unmoving where they had fallen earlier. A couple of metres away, a large metal canister lay open on its side. This apparently was what they were delivered in. I now had to complete the task of transferring them into the glass tank.

"Don't damage them, please!" Kang had begged.

From a corner cupboard Kang had described I took out and put on a pair of thick elbow-length rubber gloves and wrap-around goggles.

"Come on, boys, it's tank time!" I cried at the motionless pink and grey layer.

Kang had advised me to move only one sphere at a time. I picked one up and it slid from my fingers straight back onto the floor. I tried again, but the thick gloves made my fingers too clumsy for the job. If I held them more tightly, I might risk damaging the little bastards.

Only one thing for it. I peeled off the gloves and picked up a sphere. The revolting feel of it made me nauseous. To make matters worse, it began to pulse in my grasp. I placed it gingerly in the glass box and its motion instantly ceased. I looked at my hand and noticed a new crop of those small red marks. Apparently, there were over a hundred of the vile spheres to move; I dreaded to think what state my hands would be in when they were all safely stowed.

It took me over two hours to finish my horrible job. I stopped several times to wash my hands in one of the lab sinks. As instructed, I'd activated the air-tight plug. On the accumulated water floated a pink scum that I assumed included some of my blood. I had searched every nook and cranny of the room to make sure there were no fugitives and did indeed find one in a corner. After gratefully depositing this last straggler, I fitted the tight lid on the tank and activated its air supply.

Despite my hands resembling pieces of raw meat, the hand pad recognised me as an Alternate Palm again and Reestablished Containment once more.

I hoped I would never have to go back into that room of horrors.

I was wrong.

The Man Behind The Curtain

The discarded oxygen tank rested beside Kang's bed. He lay motionless on his side and I feared he was dead. I was relieved to see he was breathing, and he looked deeply asleep. Of course, he might be unconscious. Should I call for an ambulance? I sat on a chair and asked myself that for an age.

With the crisis passed, my decisiveness had evaporated. I felt incredibly weary and also rather cold so went to my room and got properly dressed. I also gave my hands another serious washing, though the red marks already seemed to be fading. When I returned to Kang's room, I vowed that if he was still out of it, I would call for help.

The clock showed fifty minutes had passed when Kang finally stirred. Groaning, he raised his head slightly and quizzed me about my assignment in the lab, looking relieved at my answers. Then he slumped back and closed his eyes.

More agonising time passed as only his shallow breathing

showed that he was alive. Nearly two hours later his eyes opened, and he gasped that he needed to go to the bathroom. I supported him as he made the slow journey across the room and waited until his weak call summoned me for the return trip to the bed. He was now wearing a bathrobe and his neatly folded clothes were on the bathroom floor. The effort had clearly exhausted him, and as soon as he lay down, he lapsed back into sleep yet again.

I was seriously worried that Kang was going to die, leaving me to report his death and try to explain what the hell was going on in his laboratory. I'd often wondered just who he was keeping his work secret from? Perhaps I was about to find out. My reluctant vigil was fretful as I sat on a bedside chair but frequently rose to pace the room like an expectant father in a TV show cliché.

The still brief spring daylight was starting to fade when Kang revived again. With my help he managed to sit upright, propped on a couple of pillows. My taut shoulders relaxed a little as the prospect of his imminent demise receded.

He slowly drank from the glass of water I had put beside his bed, then began speaking, softly and pausing often for breaths.

"I owe you many explanations, Joe."

"Do you think?" I replied. "You can start by telling me what's happened to your voice."

It had gradually dawned on me that since we had left

the lab, Kang had been speaking fluent English with a faint American accent and NOT SHOUTING. He didn't sound at all like the Kang whose apartment I had been sharing.

"Kang is a persona I adopted to conceal my identity. There are people…and organisations who would stop my work, and I can't allow that to happen."

"This is work involving those monsters I just cleared up?"

"Yes. It is a scaled organic simulation of the Covid-19 virus. A revolutionary way of evaluating the virus so that the whole coronavirus family may be neutralised."

I suddenly realised why those gruesome ping-pong things looked familiar. "And its initials are 'S.O.S.'? Are you kidding?" I responded.

He gave a wry smile. "Just a coincidence. This is a deadly serious. Covid-19 is likely to be followed by other and possibly worse pandemics. When I hear politicians say it's a 'once in a century' plague, I know that is a political statement. They have seen the research, yet it suits them to lie about it."

"So, who are you really?" I asked.

"I told you, my identity must be concealed," he replied.

"Oh yeah. You could tell me but then you'd have to kill me, eh?" I retorted.

In deadly earnest he answered, "No, but others might

make sure both of us disappeared."

My scepticism must have shown in my expression as Kang tried to elucidate.

"One day soon there will be vaccines created to combat Covid-19. Do you think that everyone will welcome them?'

"Of course!" I replied. "Why wouldn't they?"

Kang sighed and said, "You will find that many people will be afraid and angry. It is the nature of humanity. Some will react with violence. My own work will also meet institutional resistance. Large corporations and even governments will be set against me. That is why I must work in the shadows."

This must be the worst nightmare ever, I told myself.

I was about to give myself a slap to try and wake up when Kang spoke again. The effort of our brief conversation had obviously exhausted him, and he looked worse than ever.

"I'm sorry, Joe, but I must rest again," he gasped.

"What about those things?" I asked, pointing toward the lab.

"They will not be a problem now; at least until I start working with them. We are safe."

He then made me promise to get some rest and to wake him, if necessary, in no more than two hours.

I was too tired to argue. After asking if he needed help, which he declined, I went back to my room and fell asleep fully clothed on the bed.

Back Story

The alarm I'd set on my phone woke me from an all-too-brief sleep. Rubbing my eyes, I went to Kang's room and opened the door, suddenly panicking about him having relapsed while I slept.

He was in fact awake and had even managed to prop himself up in bed. I took this as a good sign. He still looked very fragile, although the marks on his face and hands had lightened considerably.

I had left him a bedside jug of water to go with his glass, which I was glad to see he had been drinking from. Kang beckoned me over to the chair and said, "Can I try to explain the situation to you, Joe?"

"How heavily redacted will your explanation be?" I challenged.

"I will tell you as much as I can," he promised.

It took a good half-hour without interruption for me to hear Kang's story, even though he had clearly left out anything that would provide a clue to his real identity. What was clear was that he was very wealthy and an expert in epidemiology and related fields. He was hiding in plain sight in London conducting his revolutionary research into coronaviruses and how to protect humanity from them.

He had started many months before Covid-19 appeared in China, but the spiralling pandemic had galvanised him. He repeated that unidentified enemies could stop his work (and maybe him) if they knew where he was.

"Some mock me for my 'old school' approach to research," Kang explained. "I believe that many discoveries are missed because scientists are detached from their work by sophisticated technologies. That is why I sometimes like to get literally hands on with what I am examining. Who is right? We will see."

Along the way Kang revealed that the lady whose picture was the screensaver on his laptop was his late wife. He didn't disclose her name, but her beautiful feline companion was Millie, a Maine Coon, apparently.

"Both gone now," Kang said sadly.

I felt sorry for him, which must have shown in my expression as he responded with a rare piece of personal disclosure.

"When I met my wife, I was a heavy smoker. She soon developed the habit too and a few years after we married she was diagnosed with lung cancer. It killed her. Poor Millie just pined away and in a few months she died too, of a broken heart I think. Mine was shattered, and after that terrible last year, watching my dearest struggling to breathe, I wondered if I could go on. Then I realised that by shifting my field of work a little I could help combat the growing threat to everyone from coronaviruses. The world had become complacent after the SARS outbreak but I was sure that much deadlier versions would eventually follow. So many people would hear their loved ones gasping their last desperate breaths."

It was in his wife's memory that he had devoted his life to defending us all.

"Sadly, I am too late to prevent Covid-19 but if my work succeeds there will never be another disaster like it."

When he had finished his account, he took some slow breaths. I felt he had got something off his chest that perhaps nobody else knew about.

Kang looked at me expectantly. I understood he wanted some response, but I had no idea what to say. The situation was stranger than I had ever dreamt.

Eventually I asked the questions that had been in my mind since I saw the listing for his too-good-to-be-true room what seemed like a lifetime ago.

"So why do you need a tenant and why me?"

"I was lonely," he immediately and surprisingly replied. "I don't like being isolated and on my own all the time. I thought

I could take it, but the pressure was too great. I just wanted someone around; not to be a friend or hang out with, just another human being going about their normal life."

"And to stop your little monsters from killing you," I added sarcastically.

"It was in my mind that there might be some small risk from the subjects," he admitted. "A palm impression was taken during your tenant assessment and programmed into the reader as a precaution."

"I wondered what that palm scanning business was about," I replied. "And by the way, what's with having a palm sensor for the left hand on the right side of the door?"'

Kang chuckled. "Mistake by the builders. Sometimes the simplest answer is the right one."

"You took a big risk keeping me in the dark. Just as well I could get in, eh?" was my cynical response. "So why choose Joe Dunne as your stooge?" I then asked, annoyed that I had been so naive.

"Well, you had recently been infected with Covid-19 so had some immunity. I didn't want to be nursing you or even worse calling an ambulance. I have had the disease myself and it is vicious in these outbreak stages."

I'd already worked out that my heavy dose of flu in the spring must have been Covid. Early adopter again.

Kang went on to list my other qualifications as if quoting from a report. "A suitable personality: self-contained but can be amenable; highly task-focused and driven so unlikely to be nosing around; low sociability so won't have friends over."

He went on. "Intelligent on arts/social side but mediocre on science so won't understand my work even if he stumbles across it. Plateaued in career and will likely depend on the offered accommodation for the foreseeable future," he concluded, then added, "Has an unconscious sense of social responsibility so likely to help in an emergency."

It wasn't as if I was unused to assessing people or indeed being profiled myself, yet somehow this dispassionate analysis depressed me. Far from being the main character in my own drama I seemed more like a rather dull background player.

The 'plateaued' bit really hurt, but the bitter truth was that the vampires at People People Inc were always going to leach away my ideas and energy, then cast me out eventually. I imagined Grumpus shaking his head and saying, "I tried to set your feet on the right path but just like your father you've taken the road to nowhere. Clogs to clogs in three generations."

I don't know how long Kang and I then sat in silence until he said quietly, "I'm sorry. That must have sounded harsh. I'm not as blunt as Kang, but, as my wife always said, it's lucky I didn't set my heart on being a diplomat."

His expression changed as he prepared to speak again. Something about it told me that the next thing Kang was going to say would reset my whole life. I felt terrified, but excited.

Turning Point

"There is another delivery coming tonight," Kang announced.

"What! More of those pink monsters?" was my shocked response.

"No," he answered. "Part of the same experiment, but these new simulants are dangerous."

"Hah! Not as cuddly as the pink ones, eh?"

I could guess what was coming next. "I am too weak to deal with this, Joe. I will have to ask for your help."

"NO WAY!" came my infuriated answer. "Just get the delivery postponed until you can receive it yourself."

"This cannot be done. Operators on the Dark Web are not known for their customer service, I'm afraid."

My stomach muscles clenched, and my skin crawled at the thought of being near Kang's grisly creations. I resolved not to expose myself to any more risks with them.

Kang must have read my expression as he quickly repeated his request for help before I could speak. He added, "You could help to save millions of lives by making this one sacrifice."

"So you say," I shot back. "What's some possible benefit in the future that might never happen compared to me definitely putting myself in danger now?"

He looked despairingly at me as if he was about to give up, and in a soft voice asked, "Have you ever lost someone you loved to an illness or accident you were powerless to prevent? What if you could go back in time with the ability to cure them; wouldn't you do it?"

My first thought was of my dad coming back from Africa, a sickly and distant stranger. Then, like an alarm going off inside my head, I heard Maddy's father saying, "I am afraid that she is very ill with Covid."

During a long silence broken only by Kang's laboured breathing I could almost physically feel something change in my brain. It was as if synapses were disconnecting and reconnecting themselves, closing down long-established neural paths and opening up new ones.

"Tell me what I need to do," I said.

Kang shuddered and I put my hand on his shoulder as he wept with relief. When his tears had ceased, he began to tell me what was coming next. By the time he had finished I felt like an ostrich that was wondering where that nice head-sized hole in the sand had got to.

Commitment

At four o'clock the next morning I stood in the hallway awaiting the mysterious delivery. I felt far too wound up to be tired and as scared as I'd ever been in my life.

The door buzzer rang exactly on time, but I still jumped in alarm. I nearly toppled down the stairs as my legs were so shaky. When I opened the door, a hulking figure stood outside. He was masked and it occurred to me that criminals must be having a field day now that everyone wore masks. He also wore wrap-around shades that must have made driving difficult.

"Where is the buyer?" he barked. "The package is for him only." He had a faintly central European accent.

"He's very sick. We think it might be Covid," I improvised.

The man took a step back at this, so I reassured him that I'd already had it so was not infectious.

"I will give you the package," he said grudgingly and stepped right up so we were face to face before hissing, "If you steal this, I will find you, kill you and mess your body up so that your own mother will not recognise your corpse."

I was so hysterical with terror now I nearly giggled at his threat, but I managed to control myself and held out my hands. I only needed one as the container was small compared to the cannister for the first batch. I kept my eyes on the stranger as he walked to a powerful-looking motorbike, mounted it and rode away.

As soon as he was gone, I opened the front door, hurled myself through it and locked it behind me. I sat on the bottom stair before I could fall over, noticing my white knuckles on the hand gripping the small but sinister vessel.

I opened the door into Kang's room intending to show him that the delivery had arrived, but he was fast asleep. He looked pale and drawn but his breathing sounded more normal than before.

Opening the lab door still didn't wake him up so I decided to let him sleep on. I had been thoroughly briefed about my task, so all I had to do was not screw it up.

The automatic lighting in the laboratory was on and the door slid shut behind me. I looked at the tank containing the pink/grey spheres; they were in rug mode again but gently rippling as if ready to spring into action.

Following Kang's instructions, I rummaged around the floor until I found another, smaller, transparent tank. Kang had described these containers as indestructible. I hoped he was right. I put it on a different counter from the larger tank and turned a valve on the top to the open position.

Now for the tricky bit. I inverted the canister. To my relief, its top screwed onto the tank's valve. Once the join was as tight as I could make it, I unlocked and pulled a lever on the canister. The instructions printed on the side were in Cyrillic script, so I was working from an English version in Kang's scrawled writing. I hoped that nothing had been lost in translation. There was an encouraging hiss that denoted a seal being broken and then…nothing.

As usual, Kang had given me as little information as possible about what I was doing. "Just follow my instructions," he'd pleaded. "Above all, do not let anything out of the canister unless it goes straight into the tank, and DON'T TOUCH THEM!"

At this point the new simulants were supposed to drop into the tank, except they didn't.

I waited and waited, but nothing emerged from the top receptacle. I stupidly began trying to talk them down. "Come on, guys. Lovely tank waiting for you. You don't want to be stuck in the dark when you could be looking around the nice laboratory. You've even got some mates over here!"

I wondered over to the large tank and was about to request the pink/grey inmates' help for want of a sensible tactic. I gave the indestructible glass a tap, and this set the rug to rippling more vigorously as if in readiness for round two of its fight for freedom.

Suddenly there was a rushing noise behind me. I turned and saw that the newcomers had decided to join the party. The smaller tank now contained its own freaky occupants. These were acidic green and much smaller than the resident monsters. They were also covered in sharp-looking spikes rather than nobbles. They had plastered themselves to the side facing the other tank and clung there as if ready for a bundle with the incumbents.

I belatedly remembered an instruction of Kang's I had not followed. There was a big and very thick metal screen leaning against one of the walls. As directed, I now slotted and secured it directly in front of the greenies' tank. I can't believe that they had any way of seeing their pink enemies but somehow the barrier must have blocked out their sense of the other simulants and they gradually subsided.

Having hopefully reduced the risk of a ping pong gang war breaking out I resealed the canister as per my orders and unscrewed it from the tank. I then put it in a heavily locked steel cupboard.

Kang had been insistent: "DO NOT check if there is anything left in the canister! If any remain, they will perish eventually outside of the tank environment."

I was happy to leave any stragglers to their fate and left the lab hoping that nothing would go wrong before I had some badly needed kip.

I checked on Kang as I passed his bed. I found him asleep and maybe looking a little better. I found some paper and wrote a note, which I stuck to his headboard.

MISSION ACCOMPLISHED. ONLY WAKE ME UP IN AN EMERGENCY!

I then slumped my way to bed for another bout of fully clothed sleeping.

An Offer I Couldn't Refuse

When I woke up the bedside clock registered a shocking 11.00. This was the latest I had woken up in years, and I felt irrationally guilty about it. However, I decided that as my body had just been threatened by warring green and pink viruses, it might be appropriate to indulge myself in a very long shower. It felt so good!

I slowly towelled myself dry and put on trackies, a threadbare Manchester Metropolitan University sweatshirt and some hotel-style slippers that Kang insisted be worn around the flat as opposed to bare feet. I hardly ever slopped around in stuff like that but today I decided to indulge myself.

My first, anxious priority was to check on Kang, but to my relief and surprise I heard him moving around in the kitchen. He was sitting down when I walked in and wearing a bathrobe that had probably been hand-sewn by Italian craftsmen from the highest-grade dove grey cashmere. Instant dressing gown envy. I wondered if I could claim one in return for my virus-wrangling duties.

“How are you doing? I asked him, noting that he looked a lot better if not quite the picture of health.

“I am feeling stronger, Joe,” he replied. “Some much-needed rest and above all seeing that you have transferred the new simulants successfully. I cannot thank you enough for that.”

“The new ones are mean-looking little gits, aren’t they?” I commented.

“In Korea we have a saying that you also have in England, Joe: set a thief to catch a thief. Please remember it.”

I could tell that this cryptic clue was all I would be told about Kang’s project just now, but that suited me fine.

Kang offered to make me a coffee, insisting he was up to the task if I didn’t mind waiting. Moving around slowly and stopping for an occasional sit-down, Kang meticulously made us each a large espresso. The first sip suggested a second career as barista awaited him if the mad scientist gig didn’t work out.

We sat for a while in silence, relishing our superior beverages. It seemed kind of normal in a mad abnormal way. My mind had gone into a sort of standby when Kang suddenly interrupted my reverie.

“Joe, I’m going to say something that may surprise you,

but please reflect before you respond. I want to make you an offer."

Kang's offer was pretty simple. What he wanted from me was to continue to be a housekeeper, but for the entire apartment, including the laboratory. Implied too was that, as if we were characters in a Jane Austen novel, I'd be his paid 'companion'. There might be some minimal lab assistant duties too but by and large he wanted me to steer clear of his work. Indeed, I would need to be satisfied only with the details Kang chose to share with me about that. No prying would be tolerated.

In the same secret squirrel vein, I was forbidden to try and find out anything about him. I didn't reveal that I'd already had a go at discovering his identity and found he'd covered his tracks very well.

In return for my duties, I would keep my lovely ensuite room rent free. I was welcome to share cooking and meals if I so wished. I did wish. I was a competent cook of simple stuff but having seen the meals that Kang prepared for himself – in contrast to his disgusting beverages – I expected I'd be eating very well. I would also be free to develop my consulting business, though obviously there would be no meeting clients at home and the good old PO box would have to be my business address.

I ran through various pros and cons of the deal I'd been offered. It extended beyond lockdown, which Kang predicted would last about three months. He added a further forecast that this might not be the only time the country would be shutting its doors. He didn't stipulate any end date to the arrangement, but he suggested I should assume it would be at least a year. Either of us could terminate the 'contract' with a month's notice. The timeframe was an undoubted pro, giving me the opportunity to settle into a post People People and post Liz phase but without tying me down for the long term.

I still had a question for Kang that had been bugging me for some time. I'm not sure it had any bearing on whether I accepted his offer but I just had to ask him.

"Kang, why did you decide to come to London to do your work?"

Kang hesitated, as I expected he might. Would my somewhat out of left field question be a disclosure too far? To my surprise he answered it.

"My wife's family lived in London for a few years when she was a child and she fell in love with the place and the rest of the country. We came here for a couple of short trips but she always wanted us to have a long vacation in the city and for me to see some more of Britain. Perhaps she thought I might also become enamoured, but I was always too busy for a long visit. I know it sounds silly, Joe, but I'm here because I never made that commitment to her."

I was touched by Kang's candour and, somewhat impulsively, told him I wanted to accept his offer. He shook my hand and beamed at me.

He said, "Joe, I believe that one day you will look back on

today as the start of something truly worthwhile. And always remember, there is honour in trying, even if we fail"

I hoped he was right.

Kang was tired and said we would talk at length the next day but I insisted on getting his opinion about Maddy before leaving him to rest. When I had told him about her and the little I knew of her condition he looked pensive. Then he said, "Nobody fully understands how Covid-19 will play out as a pandemic, let alone what it will do to each individual who contracts it. Your friend is young and fit, but equally important she has passion for life and determination that you admire. Hope for the best, Joe, and I will hope with you."

As I lay in bed that night the events of my life over the past few weeks teemed through my mind like a slideshow on random shuffle. The end of my engagement and my job, Maddy in hospital, the (near) bar fight and Chloe's smile. Then there was everything about Kang with his flash apartment, secret alter ego, and criminal connections. Now I was his co-conspirator too. And looming behind it all was Covid, casting a fearful shadow not just over Joe Dunne but everyone. It took me a while to get to sleep.

Kang's World

It was dinner time and it was Kang's turn to cook. His cuisine had turned out to taste even better than it smelled. We'd had a false start when the first dish he shared with me nearly melted my teeth. I'm not averse to spicy food but prefer it not to be mega hot. Thereafter Kang made a separate, toned-down version of what he prepared just for wimpy old me.

Kang was a pretty low carb eater most of the time. I'd got used to plenty of vegetable only dishes and salads, but tonight he was serving one of his native specialities: bulgogi, a barbecue meat treat, accompanied by Kang's homemade kimchi, Korea's most famous vegetable dish. In their Joe-friendly state these would be stunning. I'd never eaten Korean food before meeting the maestro, but that whole sweet and savoury combination was out of this world.

We would be using the long metal chopsticks that Kang assured me were traditional in his country. I'd been on a very slow learning curve with them but could now usually get through the whole meal without dropping food down myself.

I would be drinking a nice Pinot Gris with my meal but

Kang as ever was on water. However, this wasn't just any water, as the advert goes. His mineral water was called Jeju Samadasoo, which he bought from somewhere called Seoul Plaza in Charing Cross Road. He claimed it tasted better than any other water in the world, though I detected an element of bias in this judgement.

"The gym needs a clean tomorrow, please," Kang said as he sauntered into the kitchen.

He was aglow from his early evening exercises. Kang had revealed the flat's large and lavishly equipped workout space, concealed behind the living room at the start of our new arrangements, and it was duly added to my housekeeping roster. I had also been invited to use it. I politely declined. Plenty of brisk walking in the open air was my preferred way of staying fit.

At the time I'd asked him if there were any further nooks and crannies that I hadn't seen yet. Apparently not, though I occasionally wondered if perhaps he had a helicopter pad on the roof, ready for a swift escape.

Now, when I cook, I prefer to do it in splendid isolation. When Liz and I had the flat she was clear that any catching up on the day's news had to wait until the food was on the table. Kang, in contrast, was at his chattiest with a steaming pot or pan before him.

"I am going to upgrade the cross trainer soon," he volunteered, apropos of nothing.

This was my cue to ask a question I had long pondered. "Who does all the work on this amazing crib of yours, Kang?"

My host seemed to consider my question as he carefully cut a steak into thin strips. He frowned and I thought that this was going to be one of our many no-go zones, but he slowly began to explain, "There are people who provide places, goods and services for those of us who wish to, er, hide in plain sight."

"Like criminals?" I cheekily prompted.

He looked and sounded deadly serious as he replied, "Yes. I am not a typical customer for these hidden organisations. I try to avoid anybody who is directly involved in serious crime, but these people operate in secrecy by their nature."

"That's serious crime as opposed to comic crime?" I challenged, slightly getting on my moral high horse.

Kang stopped slicing, put the knife down and turned to me. "I make compromises. I do that for a cause that I believe in, but with each one I agonise about whether I am doing the right thing. Sometimes I just can't tell, so I live with the uncertainty. I wish you well in your life, Joe, and I hope you will never face the same dilemmas I do."

"Don't forget the delivery tonight!" Kang added, in a business-like tone that signalled we were moving on from a difficult subject.

"Aye, aye captain!" I saluted back, joining him in the

voyage to safer conversational waters.

The delivery Kang referred to was a relatively innocuous one, a weekly one-shot cornucopia of food, household goods and anything else we needed. It was sourced from various retailers, from Seoul Plaza to Fortnum and Mason, but arrived in an unmarked black van. It came every Wednesday at midnight, and it was now my job to meet it and transfer the bounty inside. The driver was thankfully not the threatening Russian purveyor of deadly ping pong balls. He was a bit surly but never threatened to do me bodily harm even if I was a bit slow carrying in the heavier boxes he handed to me.

Crisis of Confidence

Two hours! This was becoming a habit. What had happened to sleep-like-a-baby Joe Dunne, who used to leap out of bed refreshed and renewed after eight hours of unbroken kip? I'd just spent another restless night tossing and turning or staring at the invisible ceiling.

My mind kept coming back to one fundamental question: what is the point of Joe Dunne? Only days ago, I had rock solid answers to that question but they'd all crumbled to dust in my hands. In a way Julia had been right about my façade. Recent events had cracked the shell open. As a result I felt strangely liberated but also very vulnerable. Would this cocktail of excitement and anxiety prove intoxicating or toxic?

Kang had installed blackout blinds and curtains in every room so my phone was the only indicator that dawn must be breaking over London. I gave up the struggle to snooze and wearily dragged myself out of bed.

'WHAT JOE DOES NEXT.' I had created a new document with this heading over an hour ago. When I had finally given up trying to get back to sleep, I showered, shaved and dressed, then sat down at my laptop and typed those words. It was an exercise I'd used successfully in the past to kickstart some thinking about my future. It wasn't working this time.

My mind was usually buzzing with ideas, possibilities and plans. It had been like that since I was a kid, but today… nada. I'd dredged up a few thoughts but they were all variations on redundant past themes. I had never realised what a rut I was in.

Eventually I typed 'GETS LUCKY!' on the page and out of habit saved the page. Maybe inspiration would strike after breakfast.

"Joe, I will need your help in the lab later today," Kang said after I had finished my coffee and toast.

Unusually for that strange Mediterranean-style first pandemic summer in England, it was raining heavily. I wasn't planning a walk, but the idea of more lab work was not high on my list of alternative pastimes. After my shocking introduction to the room, I always dreaded going in there to clean it. Still, that was the deal and what Kang was attempting was important, so with the best grace I could muster I nodded my assent. I also resolved to do without lunch at the prospect of more ping pong encounters.

Lab-coated and gloved, Kang and I stood on opposite sides of the big work island.

"This should be the end of stage one, Joe," Kang muttered, as if I had some idea what his plan was and how many stages were in it, which I didn't.

Between us was a smaller version of the fish-tank-like containers that housed the pink and green simulants. The thick screen was still in front of the green guys to stop them sensing the pink ones and getting overexcited. Both sets of creatures were inert at this point but the mere sight of them set my teeth on edge.

Kang asked me to get one of the pink lot out and put it in the smaller tank. I did so, having practised by moving overripe tomatoes around the kitchen with the gloves on. I could see that both containers had a few centimetres of colourless liquid at the bottom. Mister Pink lay still in his new receptacle, but I put the glass top on the container as instructed.

Very carefully, Kang extracted one of the greens from its tank. He was using a pair of tongs for this job, and his quarry twitched in their grasp. These vibrations increased once it passed the screen, and Kang struggled to keep hold of it as he neared the small tank. I took off the top, noticing some movement from its pink occupant.

Kang thrust the green simulant into the small tank and I quickly shut it tight. Instantly, the newcomer rolled toward the pink ball and seemed to expand and envelope it. I almost felt sorry for the victim as it was ripped apart and seemingly absorbed. I assumed this was good news, but Kang wasn't high-fiving me yet. He watched the green victor intently. For my part I made a mental note to skip dinner too.

One of the wall clock displays in the lab was a sort of

oversized stopwatch. Kang had set it running the instant the two simulants made contact. It showed just over two minutes had passed when things began to go wrong. One of the spikes on the green simulant began to turn black, then another, and in under thirty seconds the whole thing looked like a spiky piece of charcoal.

Gingerly, Kang opened the lid a crack and poked the black mass with a long metal probe. It reminded me of one of the metal chopsticks that Kang favoured, and I thought maybe I would just stop eating for good. When he pushed with some pressure the now obviously defunct simulant simply fell apart.

Kang put the lid back on the tank and resealed it. Then he turned on his heel and walked to the lab door.

"Come on," he instructed.

I followed like the obedient lab rat I tried to be. Containment was duly established, and without speaking Kang stalked through his bedroom and on into the living room. Again, I trailed after him. He sat heavily on one of the armchairs and put his head into his hands. Suddenly he sat up and brought both fists smashing down on the coffee table, screaming, "That's it. I'm done!"

I had never seen Kang truly angry, rather than faking it in his KANG! Persona, but he was raging now.

"I was a fool to think I could succeed!" he continued. "All this time wasted for nothing." He paused, then in a quiet voice said, "I feel defeated."

When I was a psychology student, I did all sorts of different modules; some I approached enthusiastically, others less so. Among the latter was one on counselling. I couldn't see where the skill set fitted into my plans. I had no intention of becoming a social worker! However, the woman who ran it was brilliant. She made the whole class see how counselling was a universal approach that could come in handy anywhere. I knuckled down and gave it the good old college try. Apparently, I was a natural. My tutor said, "You could do this professionally if you stuck with it, Joe." No thanks!

In the years since my counselling module, I had used my listening talent in a largely self-interested way, trying to pick up information I could use to my advantage. Sitting in a chair in front of Kang, I resolved to use my rusty skills as purely as I could.

A good counsellor doesn't give much advice. Above all, they give you their full and undivided attention. They try to understand what you are thinking and, above all, feeling. That's what I did, and Kang poured out his frustrations, shattered dreams, tragedies and despair. I walked the thorny path with him, metaphorically holding his hand.

Gradually, Kang's mood began to level out. He started to express his current feelings and dilemmas as if he was talking to himself. He'd harboured great hopes for the experiment that had just failed. It felt as if all his efforts had run into an unscalable wall. I wanted to exhort him not to give up. What about all that 'there is honour in trying, even if we fail' stuff? But I stayed off my own agenda and resolutely stuck with his.

To my surprise, I realised that I'd been listening to Kang continuously for two hours and I think I'd probably been in need of a pee for the whole of the second one. Kang had lapsed into a reflective silence by now but as I excused myself, he put his hand on my arm and quietly said, "Thank you, Joe."

The next morning Kang was back at work. I sat at my desk, opened the previous day's document and added, 'HELPS GOOD PEOPLE TO DO GREAT THINGS.'

Independence Day

The interminable weeks of the first lockdown were bathed in twilight for me. The daytime of my old life hadn't quite faded but the shadows were starting to engulf it. Some evenings I still occasionally found myself wondering what I should wear to work the next day or absently began dialling Liz or Maddy for a chat. At those times I would shake my head as if to dislodge the old habits.

The news on Maddy was relatively good. When I first saw her father's number on my phone again, I was filled with dread and feared the worst. The poor man was sobbing as he told me she was finally off the ventilator, even though he must already have told lots of people before me. My own voice sounded a bit shaky as I thanked him for letting me know and asked him to give her my love.

By the middle of a sun-drenched June, the rhythm of normal life in London was tentatively quickening. Most shops were open and there were quite a few people and a good deal of traffic on the streets of west London. Everyone looked a bit wary though, as if they were doing something illicit. Lots of masks were in evidence as the government had now decided they were a vital part of combatting the virus.

Undeterred by the still slightly post-apocalyptic atmosphere outside, I strode around west London for a couple of hours each day. Hyde Park was on my map now and various spots on the Thames. I was starting to feel at home in my London neighbourhood. I felt lonely, though. Kang hardly ever left the flat as far as I knew, so my sightseeing was a solitary affair.

I often walked past KYPRO, its doors locked and windows shuttered. I wondered if it would ever reopen. There were rumours that lots of businesses had folded during lockdown as their income ceased while their overheads continued. Then on one of my walk-bys signs appeared saying *We Will Be Open Again On 4th July! All 'Independence Day' Cocktails Half Price!!* I guessed I would be able to fit a visit into my calendar.

Before lockdown KYPRO had opened at six in the evening. When I looked out of my window around five o'clock on the Fourth of July it was closed, but some tables and trendy but uncomfortable-looking seats had been positioned on the pavement in front of the bar. The backs and legs of the latter were decorated with beaten metal climbing roses; a definitive triumph of form over function. Only one chair was occupied. Relaxing on it, despite the unfit-for-purpose design, was Conor's allegedly flirtatious sister, Chloe. She was casually dressed in jeans and a chambray shirt that probably matched those stunning eyes I remembered, but that were currently concealed by sunglasses. She was sitting with her legs stretched out and her head tilted up to catch the afternoon sun.

Should I go over to the bar and say hi? I'd never been 'backward in coming forward', as old folks in Manchester say, when it came to approaching women I fancied. I'm no Ryan Reynolds but I'm okay-looking and have a certain "jaunty charm", as Maddy describes it. But for some reason the prospect of approaching this woman I'd spoken to for all of two minutes made me feel bashful.

After several minutes of agonising, I suddenly imagined Grumpus, who could not tolerate prevarication, bellowing, "Stop dithering and get on with it, lad!" in my ear. Pausing only to brush both hair and teeth, I ventured out.

The traffic was definitely lighter than on a pre-lockdown evening. I also had a sense that driving standards had slipped for some reason, as cars braked sharply and horns sounded frequently. I threaded my way through a minor gridlock and arrived in front of the recumbent Chloe.

"Well, if it isn't Mister Joseph Dunne!' she said without changing her pose at all. I was surprised she'd seen me coming and amazed she remembered my name. Her voice was slightly huskier than I recalled and her soft Irish accent made it even more enticing.

"None other," I replied. "And you are the one and only Chloe, as I recall. How are you and Conor doing?" I always made a point of remembering faces and names, so I wasn't going to be outdone.

"Pull up one of these bum-numbing items, watching out for the stupid roses, Joe, and shoot the breeze, why don't you," she invited, taking off her shades, and yes, those eyes were as alluring as I recalled.

It turned out that the wild last night before lockdown had been a Covid super spreader at KYPRO. She and Conor had both developed symptoms in the following week. She had got off fairly lightly but Conor had not been so lucky. He had not been hospitalised but even now he wasn't fully recovered. I explained that I had been a Covid early adopter and sympathised. I would tell her about Maddy when I knew her better.

"My bro is on the mend, thank goodness," she said. "But I told him I'd hold the fort here till he's a bit stronger. I've got a couple of muckers from college to help me out for cash in hand. Term's practically over now and anyone who is staying in London is looking for a side hustle or three. So, we are all set to quench our regulars' thirst if they show up in numbers."

"What if they don't?" I asked, already feeling a little anxious about KYPRO closing down and Chloe no longer being around the corner.

"Sure, the lad who owns it doesn't care if the bar loses money. He's an oligarch's son and this is just one of his toys. He **does** insist the place stays open, though, come hell or high coronavirus. Conor wanted to close way before the lockdown but the owner said keep it open or find another gig."

I found myself feeling remarkably grateful to the profligate scion of mother Russia for keeping Chloe in my orbit. Unfortunately this hadn't made me any less tongue-tied with the object of my affections. Fortunately she decided to break the slightly awkward silence.

"So, Joe, you're a bit of a mystery man yourself, aren't you?" Chloe commented out of the blue. "What's your story?"

Before I could open my mouth, she looked at her watch and said, "Rats! I've got to make sure my lackeys have the place open for business. Are you coming in for that drink we owe you?"

I nodded enthusiastically and followed her inside. As it turned out, the locals did indeed appear in great numbers for KYPRO's reopening and Chloe was run off her feet. After an hour propping the bar up, I caught her eye and signalled I was going.

She came over to me and said, "Sorry, but it looks like we'll be rammed for the rest of the night. I'd love to pick up our conversation again, though. I can be sitting outside by four tomorrow if you're around?"

"I'll be waiting," I said with unconstrained enthusiasm.

"Have you got far to go home?" she asked, ignoring the clamour at the bar.

I pointed to the cinema and she whistled.

"Wow!" she said. "A character from a movie steps down off the silver screen to sweep a simple colleen off her feet."

She winked then turned to the nearest customer. I'd only had one beer but my knees wobbled on the way home.

The Course of True Love…

For the next few weeks, I lived for my afternoon rendezvous with Chloe. We chatted about everything and nothing. We laughed and sometimes we wept. Everything about her fascinated me. Her life in Dublin, her vast family, especially her much-loved twin, her Master's course, which I was relieved to discover had another year to run. Her mention of a big paper she was writing about Social Enterprises had me trawling the internet to learn about the subject.

As a bonus it was refreshing to talk to someone who didn't seem to regard psychology with either suspicion or contempt – both driven by anxiety, in my experience. She'd touched on the subject in her own studies and seemed keen to understand it better.

Chloe wanted to hear about my life as well. I was embarrassed as I told her my story about how little of it showed me in a good light. What an egotistical, self-centred, grasping git I'd become. She didn't seem to mind. I felt as if she was giving me the benefit of the doubt all down the line. I hoped I deserved it.

The things she liked and loathed were sometimes similar and sometimes different to my preferences, but I felt the tides of my life were taking me toward many of her views rather than away from them.

Frustratingly for me, we didn't meet every day. For one thing Conor was fully fit and able to take the helm at KYPRO again. I occasionally popped in even when I knew Chloe wouldn't be around as I found her brother to be good company and he had time to chat on a slow night. He could even be tapped for background on his sister occasionally. One night when I had deftly (I felt) steered the conversation around to her holiday preferences, Conor looked me in the eye and said, "Joe, do you always faff around for ages when you fancy a girl?"

I was thrown by his directness and for a nano second considered saying I had no idea what he was on about. Terrible idea – faffing, or what?

"Is it that obvious?" I asked.

"It's plain as day you've fallen for my sis," he replied. "What's not clear to me is why you haven't done anything about it! That goes for my sister too. She's not usually 'backward in coming forward' as the auld codgers say back home. I think for whatever reason she's waiting for you to make the first move."

I took a deep breath. "Conor, I remember the first thing you said to me about Chloe was that she's a flirt? I know this sounds pathetic but I'm a bit beaten up emotionally right now. Mostly my own fault but, you know…"

Conor's eyes were somewhat like his sibling's but a bit lighter and nearer to the piercing end of the blue spectrum. His gaze was more direct than ever as he said, "I can't tell you what to do, Joe, nor can I speak for Chloe, but if it was me, I'd take the risk and ask her out." He then put a finger to his lip and said, "By the way, this conversation never happened."

He ended the potentially awkward moment by pouring us both a lager and clinking glasses with a hearty "Slainte."

...Never Did Run Smooth

The day after my heart to heart with Conor was one that Chloe and I had bookmarked for a potential afternoon get-together, and I was determined to ask if she would like to go out with me some time. She'd cancelled her plans to visit her family in Dublin over the summer vacation. Her gran lived with her folks and, just like my dad, she had to shield. I dreamt of spending sunny days in Chloe's company.

Conor though was off to Dublin for a scratch hurling game with some of his mates and Chloe would be in charge at the bar this fine Friday evening. The sun was shining and a throng was expected. The hours dragged their little feet from the moment I got up until what I thought would be a not-too-desperate-looking time to be waiting outside KYPRO. Well, she might be early.

I felt as nervous as a callow teenager as I made the short walk to the bar. I had just reached the pavement tables when I heard voices approaching the corner from the other side of the building.

"I don't care if he said we're barred. We're goin' to Drink Out To Help Out! I'm not letting some stroppy Mick tell me what to do."

They were the unmistakable dulcet tones of the gorilla; I assumed he had his sidekick the weasel with him.

"That's right," squeaked his mate. "Bloody Scotsman."

I dived into a shop doorway so I could gather my thoughts. As they turned the corner the gorilla spoke again.

"I promised you some Russian beer, Cousin Tommy, and as you've come all the way from 'ackney, you're gonna have it **cos I say so**!"

Then I heard a voice I didn't recognise. It was controlled compared to the others' strident trumpeting but sounded like a robot with a grudge. The words were spat out slowly rather than spoken, with unexpected pauses for effect.

"They'll be sorry if they kick off, because…we'll come back and burn the place down."

I could see the trio reflected in a side window of the shop (and hoped they couldn't see me). It was a good enough view that I picked up what looked like shock on the two locals' faces. Tommy sounded like he was in a different and more violent league from them.

I knew that Chloe might appear at any moment, so instead of dialing 999 like a smart person I stepped out from my hiding place and said, "Look, guys, you're going to get into big trouble here. Why don't you find somewhere with less bother?"

I hoped this appeal to self-interest might make them stop and think – to the extent they were capable of it.

What actually happened was that the big guy validated my earlier theory that in a sober state he could put me on the ground with one punch. He ran up to me and feinted with his right hand then smashed me in the jaw with his left. Should have remembered he was a southpaw. The proverbial sack of potatoes would have definitely gone down slower than I did, but I still had time to bash my knee on one of the uncomfortable chairs in my descent to the pavement. I knew those sharp edges were a bad idea. His weaselly friend then took the opportunity to give me a hefty kick in the ribs.

I started to get up, though my head was spinning. You know those stars they have when someone gets bashed in a cartoon? They're really a thing. My assailants let me rise while they admired their handiwork and prepared the next assault. I just hoped they finished with me before Chloe arrived. If a random police car came round the corner that would be good too.

Then Cousin Tommy pushed his way between the other two, seeming to want his own piece of the Joe Dunne beat-down. He was a tall and spindly guy in grimy jeans and a torn leather jacket. My spinning mind thought he must be quite warm in that. My head cleared quickly when he produced the knife. It was nasty-looking, 30 centimetres long at least, curved toward its wicked point and with a serrated edge.

As he walked toward me, Tommy said, in his creepy robot voice, "I'm gonna… cut 'im."

The rest of Tommy's crew took a step back when they saw the knife. I could tell this was not how they'd expected the evening to go, but Cousin Tom had his own kind of fun in mind.

Have you ever been so scared and hopeless that you stop worrying? That's what happened to me as Tommy approached. Provided Chloe was alright I didn't care what these morons did to me.

"HAHA!"

It was like a dream to hear the old Kang voice boom out. There were stomping footsteps behind me too, so maybe this was real.

"Zombie knife!" Kang 1.0 continued as he neared us. "VERY BAD!"

"Piss off, Chinky…none of your business," Tommy the robot said.

"And take your Covid with you!" chipped in the weasel.

"YOU DARE INSULT PEOPLE'S REPUBLIC OF

CHINA?!" Kang bellowed back, leaning into their national identity error.

I wondered dazedly how Kang was going to fight off three thugs with only semi-conscious me on his side. A long-buried memory of watching *The Karate Kid* slipped through my mind.

Tommy was almost beside me, but he definitely had an eye on Kang and now had the knife pointed toward him rather than me. He opened his mouth as if to speak when his adversary stepped past me and produced something that looked like a pistol from behind his back.

"Say hello to my leetle friend," said Kang, in a strange, unidentifiable accent.

I was hysterically thinking that Tommy probably wished he hadn't brought a knife to a gunfight when Kang spoke again.

"You know taser, ha?" he enquired, and Tommy's complexion immediately slipped into the Deathly White section of the Pantone chart.

"HAHA! You been shocked before!" Kang gleefully observed and I could hear the taser whining as if eager to be used.

"This is state of art," Kang proudly announced. "Biggest charge ever! Now drop knife and kick to me, yes?"

Tommy didn't hesitate as he followed my rescuer's instructions. Kang's guess about the man's previous acquaintance with tasers must have been right, as he was goggle-eyed with terror.

Kang took a handkerchief from his pocket and bent to pick up the knife by its tip.

"GOOD!" he announced, examining the knife's handle. "Many fingerprints." He pointed back at the cinema and added, "Lot of cameras on building so much film of attack. Like being in movie!"

The three former tough guys looked like they were in shock as Kang wagged his finger at them and roared, "NEVER COME BACK HERE OR YOU GO TO JAIL AND THEY THROW AWAY KEY! RUN!"

The trio instantly took to their heels. As they left, I heard the weasel say to Tommy, "Did you get that knife off Amazon?" The gorilla slapped him sharply on the back of the head in mid-stride.

As the adrenaline began to leave my system, I staggered but Kang held me up and helped me back across the road.

"What about Chloe?" I asked as we neared the flat's door.

"You don't want her to see you like this, Joe," Kang replied. "They won't be back, **ever**, and you can call her later to explain you were held up by an emergency. OK?"

I responded by blacking out.

Think On It

When I came to, I was lying on Kang's bed and he was carefully examining the aching side of my face.

Seeing that I was conscious Kang said, "That was some left hook he caught you with, Joe. Could have broken your jaw but you will be okay. Always watch out for us southpaws, eh?"

"Thanks for the advice. And thanks for probably saving my life, by the way."

As an afterthought I added, "It's a miracle that you arrived right on time, isn't it?"

Ignoring my gratitude and curiosity for the moment, Kang said, "I've examined your ribs and none of them seem to be broken. Your knee has survived too. Apart from the fact you will basically be one big bruise for a week or two you have shown great resilience."

I know when I'm being deflected so as my mind focused, I asked Kang directly, "I can't believe you just happened to be gazing out of a window and saw me being attacked. How did you know?"

Kang sighed but with obvious reluctance he admitted, "I really do have surveillance cameras on the building, Joe. Leading-edge stuff too. **South Korea, good tech!**" he added in his persona voice.

Kang explained that his system had facial recognition built in.

"When you told me about your encounter with the two thugs in the bar before lockdown, I examined the footage from that night and captured their faces. I set an alert to sound if they should ever be detected by the cameras again. It went off as soon as they rounded the corner tonight, so I hurried to the rescue."

"Handy you had a taser lying around the place," I observed.

"It's in a concealed cupboard by the door," he revealed. "I'll show you tomorrow. As you know, I have to deal with some shady characters, so self-protection is needed."

I was finding the conversation a useful distraction from my many growing aches and pains so I asked him another question. "Where are the screens for the CCTV?"

Kang shrugged and responded, "Not for you to bother about."

Resigned to my ignorance about the many byways of

Kang's Minotaur maze, I changed topics.

"By the way, what was that 'leetle friend' in the funny accent remark all about?"

"For a man who lives above a cinema your movie knowledge is sadly lacking, Joe. It's a line from *Scarface*, when Al Pacino turns a grenade launcher on the gang who are trying to kill him. Second greatest gangster movie after *Goodfellas*!"

I silently tucked gangster movies alongside horror films in my taxonomy of nasty cinema I never wanted to watch.

"Talking of surveillance cameras, won't the official ones at the road junction have captured our standoff, including you brandishing a taser?" I asked with some concern.

"Probably," Kang replied, looking relaxed. "Nobody is ever going to look at it unless a crime is reported. I am quite sure that the three thugs won't be doing that – and **nor will we**," he added emphatically.

When I moved to sit on the edge of Kang's bed, sharp pains assailed me from multiple sites on my body and I groaned loudly.

Kang walked over to the shelf where he had placed a glass of water and a bottle of pills. He retrieved them, and handing me the pills he said, "These are very strong, Joe, so I'm only giving you a few for today. Paracetamol only after that, I'm afraid, but these might help you sleep tonight."

I thanked him and turned to limp around to my room. As I did so Kang spoke again.

"So, Joe, when I appeared in the street did you think I was going to take the enemy down with some slick martial arts moves?"

I gave a sheepish nod.

Kang smiled ruefully as he commented, "That's the thing in this country; people think anybody who looks like me must be Bruce Lee."

An hour later, as I lay in bed praying for the meds to take effect, Kang's final remark had reminded me of a long-ago conversation with Grumpus. He must have heard me use a name or phrase picked up from other kids at school that showed some form of prejudice. I can't recall against whom, but there were many candidates for derision from my peers. Grumpus rounded on me.

"Dead end thinking!" he announced.

This was a favourite phrase of my grandfather's, frequently applied when talking about anything with which he disagreed. I winced at the thought of the rhetorical questions routine that was likely to follow.

"So, lad, I'm going to teach you a valuable lesson. When you're about to meet someone for the first time, there is only one question you should have in mind. It is **not**: What sex are they? What colour's their skin? Where were they born? Who, if anybody, do they pray to? Who do they like to go to bed with? **What** is the key question, young man?"

"What can they do for me?" I apprehensively replied.

"Correct answer!" Grumpus shouted and even clapped me on the back. "All those other questions are irrelevant stuff and nonsense. Now think on it!"

"Good advice, if dodgy reasoning Grumpus," I thought as I painfully turned over. "I need to keep thinking." And then I was asleep.

Hail the Hero

On Friday, when I phoned Chloe to apologise and explain why I hadn't met her I decided to keep it short and vague, just saying I'd been in 'an altercation' outside the bar.

"I wondered who'd scattered our tables and chairs around. Are you okay, Joe? You don't sound well at all," she asked in a reassuringly concerned voice.

"I'll live," I replied, trying to sound simultaneously wounded but nonchalant. "But I need to rest up for a couple of days. See you on Monday?"

Chloe was sitting outside waiting for me when I limped over to KYPRO on Monday afternoon.

"Oh my god, Joe!" she cried when she saw me. "Your poor face!"

She reached out and gently touched my bruised and swollen right cheek. Oh, that felt good; almost worth getting hit for.

Chloe insisted that we should sit in Conor's tiny office behind the bar. I gave her the somewhat edited account of Friday's battle, which Kang had consented to. The terrible trio were the culprits but the knife was omitted from the story. Kang saved the day but the taser wasn't mentioned either. I noticed that Chloe didn't once suggest that my saviour might have gone Jackie Chan on the attackers' asses. Some people don't need to be taught to 'think on it', seemingly.

Chloe explained apologetically that the bar's owner refused to install any internal or external CCTV that might have provided evidence of the attack. She looked like she was about to make a further comment but didn't speak. I didn't know her well but I guessed that she must suspect there was a lot I wasn't telling her about the events of Friday afternoon. I was acutely aware of the many gaping holes in my own narrative, such as why I hadn't reported the incident to the police.

It meant a lot to me that, instead of quizzing me about the details, she said, "Joe, when you heard those eejits coming round the corner you challenged them because of me, didn't you?"

I felt strangely bashful as I replied, "Guilty as charged, your honour."

"Oh, you lovely man," Chloe whispered as she leaned across the table and kissed me softly on the lips.

She then stood up and shouted, "Three against one! I just wish I'd come up behind them with the Louisville Slugger in me hands. They'd be eating their breakfasts through a straw now, so they would!"

Tender but fierce. That was Chloe all over. I steeled myself to ask her out.

More Than Kin

What a glorious August day! The sun was blazing down on Battersea Park and Chloe had promised to bring along a picnic feast when we went there for the afternoon. I wasn't sure how long term our relationship would be, but we were both enjoying it in the present, which was very much her style.

I was surprised and grateful at how readily Chloe ignored my many evasions and downright untruths in explaining my situation with Kang. She must have had her suspicions. It was either that she didn't care enough to probe or that she trusted me enough to believe I had benign reasons for holding things back.

We had walked past the Arts Cinema recently and the *Fear Eats The Soul* posters were gone. Instead, as part of their (optimistic seeming) autumn programme, there was a poster for *Un Bonheur N'Arrive Jamais Seul*. Like the other poster it featured a man and woman, but they looked considerably cheerier than their predecessors. When I suggested we might go to see it when the cinema reopened Chloe said, "Let's not get ahead of ourselves, huh?"

She was finally going back to Dublin at the weekend for a few days and staying with an auntie so she could see her folks and talk to her gran through the window. She promised to return with more lore on the Dunnes. Her ongoing research into my roots had us in County Wicklow, but she was convinced that we stemmed from a noble family called the O'Regans. I said if she was right I would insist on being addressed as 'Your Lordship' from now on. Her reply to this drew impressively on her glossary of Gaelic swear words. The translation made me blush.

My parents had been fascinated by the family genealogy I shared with them during my visit the previous week when shielding was paused. It was the best time we'd had together since I was a little kid. I guess we were so relieved we had all survived the pandemic thus far that a well of genuine affection had been tapped. I was sure they must have had unanswered questions about my recent past, not to mention my present and future, but decided I would give the answers (or not) when I was ready. At least the wounds from my beating were no longer visible or obvious, so that was one awkward conversation I didn't have to navigate.

My dad seemed surprised when I suggested the two of us go for a walk along the beach one evening. He probably felt wary of having our usual awkward conversation, talking at cross purposes, misunderstanding each other and so on. It was a little stilted to begin with, but as the sun began to dip toward the Irish Sea, we both relaxed.

"You seem to be happy, Joe," Dad remarked.

I nodded and he continued: "Not sure I ever saw you as a part-time housekeeper, even though you always kept your room spotless at home." (I hadn't mentioned my other duties as jobbing lab assistant.)

"I'm glad you're going to start your business again, though. I know it's mainly a commercial proposition for you, but what you encourage are just the right things to do. If only organisations and bosses treated people with compassion and respect, the world would be a better place!"

After all these years, my father and I finally had some common ground. He was delighted to hear that I now actually cared about 'the right things' for their own sake. I found it dovetailed beautifully with my passion for 'stuff that works' and I was sure to leave the dreaded plateau behind and ascend the mountains. They would be in a new direction, though.

"Dad, I've decided to concentrate my work on charities. Do you still have contacts in that world that could get me started?"

He put his arm around my shoulders for the first time since I was a youngster and said, "Son, I'd be honoured to help."

On The Mend

My next post-lockdown trip was closer to home. It was my first chance to see Maddy since the hospital had let her come home to her family the previous week. A long convalescence was predicted but hopefully a full recovery, with caveats about the unknown long-term consequences of Covid-19. I had asked her parents if Maddy would be able to handle an onscreen chat and was thrilled when they said that her daughter had demanded I get myself out to Hertfordshire pronto!

We sat in socially distanced seats on the terrace of the Velankars' beautiful garden with bracing cups of Assam tea, the house speciality, to hand. I was shocked to see how frail my old friend looked. Despite her various athletic pursuits, she had never been particularly slim, but now she was achingly thin.

"What some girls will do to get into a size ten, eh, Joe?" was her greeting. "I'd give you a big hug but you've doubtless been told to keep your distance."

"Consider it banked," I replied, then my voice cracked as I continued. "Oh God, Maddy, it's so good to see you."

"Whoah! Joseph, have you gone all sentimental on me?" she challenged.

"Long story," I managed through my tears.

"Well, begin at the very beginning," she prompted, taking a sip of her tea.

When I'd finished my lengthy and rather jumbled narrative, Maddy sat back and said, "Phew! That is an epic, Giuseppe. A bit vague on your current arrangements, but I guess you have your reasons. Now, most important of all, do you have a photo of the lovely Chloe?"

I showed her one on my phone.

"Punching above your weight again, eh?" she commented appreciatively. "I thought you said she was Irish, but that blonde hair ain't out of a bottle."

I explained that Chloe's research had shown her family to be of Dublin Viking stock.

"I like her already," Maddy concluded.

We sat in comfortable silence for a while, then Maddy began. "My own tale is a familiar one, Joe. Girl meets virus, it falls for her but just when they're getting close, she realises it has several million others on the side and kicks it out with a little help from the Royal Free Hospital."

We talked about the future. Maddy was convinced that when she could get out and about again, the long-awaited 'suitable girl' would appear and be wowed by her newly svelte body.

I commented, "I'm sure there's a lady shoemaker out there who has no idea what is going to hit her."

"Joe, you read it!" Maddy exclaimed, then went into a coughing fit.

By the time it had subsided, her mum was lurking by the door, suggesting that perhaps that was long enough for today. We said our goodbyes and I promised to visit again soon. Sitting on the train back to London I laughed and cried a bit. The man sitting opposite looked thoroughly embarrassed, but I didn't care.

I honestly had no idea if Kang's work was life-saving genius or deluded fantasy. The guy knew his stuff, though. He'd accurately anticipated the pandemic's path so far. He also had some grim predictions for the next year or two, though he forecast a vaccine arriving by the end of the pandemic's first year. His own horizon was way beyond that. I felt if there was even a chance he could forestall outbreaks of worse scourges he could count me in. I was happy to be assistant lab rat when needed. Fortunately, Attack of the Deadly Ping-Pong Balls Part Two was never made. I got the creeps whenever I went near them, though.

One week, on hearing that I would be by myself for a few days, Kang had invited me again to his movie night on Friday.

I hate to say it, but I was now something of a Harry Potter fan, having watched the first three films with Kang over the summer.

As I went into the kitchen to chill a bottle of wine, the man himself was pottering about. (Geddit?)

"Don't forget about *Goblet of Fire*," he reminded me, and as I left the room he shouted in his old Kang voice, "FIFTY POINTS TO GRYFFINDOR!"

I stopped and bellowed back, "SIXTY POINTS TO SLYTHERIN!"

Well, I couldn't go completely soppy, could I?

All The Fun

"Could you look in on the twins?" Chloe asked me. "I am assisting your cordon bleu father in creating a sort of Cantonese meze, and we're at a delicate stage with the Peking duck. Time for the sorcerer to take advice from his apprentice, I think. See what I did there?" she added and winked in that way that even after a decade together made me go weak at the knees.

Without waiting for a reply, she dived back into the steamy kitchen from which tantalising aromas seeped. My stomach grumbled at the prospect of the feast to come. Dad was a brilliant cook. When his globetrotting days were over he'd brought the world's cuisine to our kitchen. Luckily for me, my darling wife was no slouch either and together they were a culinary dream team. (I only occasionally pined for Kang's unbeatable kimchi.)

I made my way up the creaky stairs of Grumpus' old house and thought back to the days when I used to stay here. I was glad that Francis and Margaret, better known as Frank and Peggy, our seven-year-olds, could enjoy their trips to the Fylde without having to do a day of backbreaking boat maintenance.

I opened the bedroom door to see them both comatose after spending the afternoon walking along the chilly strand with us and skimming pebbles on the sea. Vixi Venus, our Dachshund, lay across them, also out of it. Draped across her in turn was my folks' small tabby and white rescue cat, Lucy. She was the benign despot who ruled the house and all its inhabitants, resident or visiting. She opened her eyes slightly, which was my signal to provide a gentle ear rub. If reincarnation was a thing, I was totally coming back as a cat. Lucy yawned to indicate that my duty was discharged, and I left the gently snoring, purring heap to their hopefully happy dreams.

As I walked onto the landing, I recalled what Grumpus always said about pets: "Scavengers, the lot of them. Only mugs'd give them house room."

The old curmudgeon would also have been infuriated by the Christmas decorations that now festooned his austere home and the beautifully dressed and lit tree in his formerly spartan living room. I couldn't remember him ever using the word 'humbug', but he didn't need to.

When I got downstairs, Mam was preparing the dinner table. She loved to make these family dinners special occasions. I was humming a non-festive tune when I arrived.

"Ah, 'Some Guys'! One of the few pop songs your grandad could stand," she observed. "Did you know that there were two records with that name? The one by Robert Palmer has the bit about having all the fun. The one Grumpus liked was

Rod Stewart's, where some guys are getting all the breaks, but others are moaning brats who have all the pain. Summed up his philosophy of life, really. He could only feel like a winner if other people were losing."

Suddenly my mind was full of Grumpus memories and words. "Do you mind if I pop outside for a bit, Mam?" I asked.

"I think I can manage here, Joe," she replied, arching an eyebrow at me. "I'm informed by the kitchen staff that the feast will be ready in half an hour."

I pulled on my heavy jacket as protection from a now biting wind off the Irish Sea and closed the back door behind me. After I had walked a few metres into the garden I turned to look back at the old house. It had always been kept in a sound but basic state by Grumpus but, thanks to my folks' loving care, it was now a welcoming and attractive home. Mam had insisted on having the exterior painted white. She overrode Dad's protests about practicality, and even he had to admit it looked lovely in its new livery. It had been named 'The Peninsula' when my grandparents bought it, but Grumpus had quickly changed that to 'Crags'. Returned to its previous identity, the grand old dame really looked the piece.

I wandered down to the end of the garden towards the wall. I could have opened the gate and walked down the slipway to the erstwhile boat mooring. Instead, my destination was the large outbuilding where Grumpus had devotedly maintained his boat. The vessel was long gone, bequeathed to the trusty RNLI on condition it was sold with proceeds going to the charity. Suitably converted, the now subdivided outbuilding was both the bustling hub of Dad's repair business and studio for Mam's live-streamed Tai Chi classes.

I unlocked the door, and the lights came on automatically. As I entered dad's workshop, I had a strange sense of son and father toiling alongside each other unaware. I had once been shown a photo taken on an old film camera that was a double exposure: one scene superimposed on an earlier one by mistake. It was a quaint and ghostly sight with the same eerie but oddly touching sense I was feeling now.

For a while I pushed thoughts of my grandfather aside and indulged in some memories of my golden decade since the events of the first Covid lockdown. My eighteen months as Kang's part-time lab assistant and housekeeper had been surprisingly enjoyable. I also thought of myself as nanny to various ping pong balls; a macabre Mary Poppins. I hoped that I was contributing in however minor a way to something that might be of benefit to humankind. Kang warned me that most attempted medical breakthroughs ended in failure and it was impossible to guarantee the success of his project.

"But there is honour in trying, even if we fail."

I was so familiar with the phrase by now I joined in the chorus.

Meanwhile, I used my remaining work time to build my consulting business with charities. I say work time because I had also chosen to get a life, and in the main that meant getting Chloe.

I had fallen for my Dublin Viking girl in a big way and fortunately, she felt the same about me. We couldn't get enough of each other, in all the right ways.

The second lockdown only intensified our relationship. We were strictly limited to meeting outside and it was the middle of winter, but you know that old song, 'I've got my love to keep me warm'? Our favourite walks were beside the mighty Thames and across its contrasting bridges. We would always stop on those and kiss passionately as the winter winds tugged at us. Somehow the fact that we wouldn't be going home together made it feel even more fiercely romantic.

The third lockdown saw the harshest restrictions return. I couldn't leave my two-person 'bubble' and I could only see my beloved on screen, even though she was just a few miles away. I told Kang I was tempted to go and see her as we had both already had Covid but he was dead set against it.

"In this situation we must all set the right example. We stand together or fall apart," he said sternly.

Once all the lockdowns were finished, my darling and I were together as much as possible. When her Master's in Business Management was coming to an end, we engaged in numerous but inconclusive discussions about what would come next. Fortunately, Kang was about to give us the nudge we needed.

I occasionally managed to persuade Kang to spend some time outside for his physical and mental health. This usually consisted of the two of us and sometimes Chloe going for a walk in Battersea Park. Kang always insisted on wearing shades, a baseball cap, and a voluminous jacket that Chloe and I ribbed him about mercilessly.

One day, when it was just the two of us, he shared with me that he would soon need to move his work to a proper laboratory and involve other experts in his field. "The risks for me will be much greater then, but I have done what I can here."

On the day I moved out to go and stay with Chloe, Kang put his arm over my shoulder and said, "Someday you will hear it announced that the Covid-19 pandemic is over. I want you to be sceptical about this. Pandemics can return several times and, in some cases, they attack groups we don't normally consider vulnerable. Take care of yourself and your family. You have much to offer the world, I think."

He then looked me in the eye and said, "I will miss the apartment and you, Joe. Your help and companionship will be forever in my heart."

I had come to see Kang as almost an elder brother due to the uplifting example he always gave me. I wanted to offer him some wise words in return before we parted, maybe forever.

"Kang, I know that you have dedicated your life to saving the world and that you shoulder its burdens without hesitation or complaint. I want you to remember that you also deserve happiness and love, my friend. When the time comes, stop and see who might be around you."

Chloe was waiting for me downstairs when I emerged from the flat, ready to go to her place. She had said her fond farewells to Kang the previous day. "Why, Joe, you're crying," she said, putting her arms around me. "Darling boy, as my wise gran always says to me: don't cry for what you've lost, smile for what you've had."

A few days later, I couldn't resist going back to see the cinema building. The door to the upstairs flat and its windows were already boarded up and I guessed the interior had been gutted so no trace was left of Kang or his work. I waved at the façade and said, "Goodbye, you funny old stick, Kang. Keep well, my hero, and save the world if you can."

Then I turned and walked away to the rest of my life with hope in my heart and Kang's cautionary words in my ears.

Vindication

As it turned out, Kang's prophecy of an unexpected, deadly Covid-19 wave came frighteningly true five years after his warning to me. The first news reports told of a minor outbreak in Mexico City. This was soon followed by others in adjacent countries, including the southern US states. As Kang had implied, the new variant was most severe among young adults and older children. It attacked their immune systems just like the terrible Spanish flu wave in 1920. Anticipated death rates in these groups were appalling. The tabloids named it the Omega variant, and we all feared that it was last but worst.

Then, as suddenly as it had started, the outbreak in Mexico died out. Patients began to recover, and the infection rate quickly dwindled to nothing. The same thing happened at all the other disease sites. Now the news reports were full of stories about a counter virus detected among infected patients. *The Sun*'s front page proclaimed, "Corona Killer Kicks Covid's Ass!"

Speculation was rife about the origin of the new virus, which seemed coincidentally to have spread in all the infection hot spots without the help of vaccination. The unexpected cure inspired gratitude and provoked resentment in equal measure. I was shocked by the level of hostility, both institutional and personal, expressed toward the unknown creator of the Covid antidote. Kang's fear of enemies at many levels seemed well founded.

A short-lived social media story implicated a mysterious 'Maine Foundation', but exhaustive searches both official and unofficial in that part of New England failed to provide evidence of secret laboratories. I felt my suspicions about the world's mysterious saviour from Covid were confirmed when one day I received an anonymous message on my phone: "ONE MILLION POINTS TO GRYFFINDOR!"

It was widely reported that the Omega outbreak was indeed the last gasp of Covid-19 and that its mysterious nemesis might also spell the end of all coronavirus infections as it spread throughout the global population. The world exhaled, and with some lessons learnt (and some not), humanity's heartbeat grew stronger.

One beneficiary of this was my soon-to-be brother-in-law Conor. He and his team had bought the KYPRO bar when the oligarch's son, frantically liquidating his UK assets after his country invaded Ukraine, wanted to sell up. Thanks to an inspired crowdfunding effort led by his brilliant sister, he had completed the buy-out with surprisingly little hassle. The place was renamed THE HURLEY and Conor's stick from his days as a hurling star had pride of place above the bar. He assured me that the baseball bat was still tucked away in case of trouble, as he didn't mind "breaking that over some eejit's head". A year later, the new entrepreneurs had been having a tough time of it and Omega had seemed likely to spell the end of their fledgling business, but in the new age of optimism the customers returned and they began to flourish.

Chloe and I were also energised by the great escape and moved to a flat in Manchester with designs on a family house in Didsbury in due course. Our wedding was in Dublin, where the Nolan hordes greatly outnumbered the Dunne contingent and Mum's Branthwaites but welcomed us with open arms.

My team was bolstered by the future Doctor Velankar, rising star of Accident and Emergency medicine. As my 'Best Mad,' she charmed the whole ensemble, especially Chloe's striking cousin Birgit. Chloe had confided in me that she hoped Maddy might hit it off with her cuz. She'd explained to my friend that the name Birgit was Scandinavian with ancient Irish roots meaning 'exalted one'. She went on to read aloud from one of her genealogy texts: "Birgit is for the baby whose eyes look upon the world with wisdom and curiosity." Yes, it was love before first sight, and a year later I was 'Mate of Honour' as my dear Maddy wed her suitable girl at last.

Conor invited Maddy and Birgit to have their wedding reception at the bar, an offer they gratefully accepted. In one of our Zoom calls to discuss the arrangements he shared some news of an old haunt with me.

"So, Joe, there's a new restaurant opened above the Arts Cinema."

After giving me a moment to take this in he asked, "You'll never guess what kind of cuisine they do?"

"Korean!" I exclaimed.

"Nah, French," said Conor with a wink as roguish as his sister's was flirtatious. "I could book you and Chloe a table there when you come down," he offered.

I momentarily pictured pink and green ping pong balls among my escargots and quickly declined.

I guess if my life hadn't been productively derailed back in '20 I might, ten years on, still be obsessed with work, but now it trickled in at the tail end of my reflections. I thought back to a pivotal early conversation with Chloe when she said emphatically, "One thing you need to know about me, Joe, is I'm not about the money. I hope to be wealthy in many ways, but chasing big bucks is not on my agenda."

If the old materialist, self-aggrandising Joe lingered anywhere in my mind that was the moment he took flight for good.

In fact, Chloe and I each built very successful and respected practices. Her ever-innovative business brain was put to work advising her beloved social enterprises on investment and borrowing strategies in line with their values; pretty cool! Some were prepared to work with both of us for a small stake in their businesses. Because, with my guidance they treated their employees, customers and each other well, they usually prospered, and we ploughed most of our dividends into the next batch of paragons.

I was unsurprised but shamefully delighted to learn that my former employers, People People Inc, had not been prospering while I flourished. I read the announcement about them closing their UK business with relish and laughed out loud when I saw a post from none other than Chuck that he was 'Looking for new opportunities and was available for interview at any time'.

When Chloe was next out of the office, I spent an hour creating a meme to send to Chuck of Dick Van Dyke as Bert saying, "Wothcher, me old china! Well, it's an unjolly 'oliday for Chucky, eh?" I deleted that and then wrote a message saying I'd sat by the river long enough to watch my enemy's body float past. With a sigh I deleted that too, deciding that the new me was above such childish vindictiveness – just.

One sticky work conversation I had with Chloe concerned 'my' algorithm or, as she framed it, the work I had shamelessly taken for nothing from one of my supposed best friends. Accountant and lawyer were quickly summoned, and a deal drawn up to pay Micky his due share of the profits generated by his contribution.

The man himself, now married to my ex, was as relaxed as ever when I called him with the news of an old wrong being righted.

"Hey, bruh, you di'nt need to do that. I always said you'd turn out dope. I know there's like stuff between us, but Christmas cards at least, okay?"

I promised and we've kept them going ever since, but

I've never had any other contact with him and Liz. We don't really live that far apart but sometimes there's just too much gone down.

To Thine Own Self

I had really enjoyed contemplating the recent good times, partly because it helped me to avoid facing a factor in my life that always lay unresolved at the back of my mind.

Having experienced my Road to Damascus moment, I had turned my back on all memories of Grumpus. I rejected my grandfather's views on life and regretted their impact on me. I especially felt remorse for the many selfish things I'd done and the way I had used other people so I could get what I wanted. How slavishly I had aped Grumpus and his creed.

After one of my rants about the old man, Chloe had demanded that I not mention him again until I could tell her something I genuinely liked about him. That had been a couple of years ago, and only now in the dusky Fylde twilight was I ready to attempt some kind of internal reconciliation.

For inspiration, I gazed out of the full-length window that looked out onto the sea. This had replaced the double doors of old that had opened onto the slipway. In an instant, I was transported back to the occasion of my first trip on the vessel he had named *My Boat*. How like the old man to shun the 'damned sentimental' idea of christening the one thing he loved. It had taken a year of school holiday toil and constant nagging for me to persuade Grumpus to take me on the boat. I think he had been testing my commitment to the cause and I had at last passed muster.

"Right! If it'll stop your grizzling you can come with me **now**." Grumpus sounded exasperated, but that was one of his favourite moods along with disgusted, irritated, and contemptuous.

"You'll be crewing as I tell you, and if I hear one complaint you're going over the side. Understand?"

I nodded vigorously, telling myself he couldn't be serious about the last bit, could he? The boat was moored at its jetty, bumping noisily against the side as we clambered aboard. My stomach's churning matched the chop of the waves as we cast off and turned onto open water.

The first part of the trip was exhilarating once I'd got used to the movement of the boat on the water and the constant slaps of spray in my face. Grumpus seemed to do little enough but still kept us on a straight course slicing through the waves. Young though I was I could appreciate his mastery of sailing. It felt like a privilege to be trusted to share this time and maybe even learn to take the helm myself someday.

As time went on, I noticed that Grumpus frequently looked at the sky, which had darkened appreciably since we set out. The wind had got stronger too, and our rise and fall were great enough to make me glad we had skipped lunch.

"When will we be going back?" I asked anxiously.

"When I say so!" he snapped.

Soon the north wind was whipping heavy rain as well as spray into our faces and I was relieved when Grumpus indicated we were going to come about and head home.

It was as Grumpus stood to adjust the sail that he fell. His head made a sickening noise as it struck the hull. The unattended boom and tiller swung wildly, but I dived and got my hands on the boom and relevant sheet just before we keeled over. I looked at my slumped grandfather and saw his eyes were closed and his temple was bleeding freely. I had no idea how to steer the boat other than to copy what I had seen Grumpus do to keep us moving forward. So that's what I did, heading us ever further out to sea and into the teeth of the storm. It was a big boat and it took all my boyish strength to keep it on a straight course.

As the sea got rougher, I became convinced I was going to die. Grumpus had often regaled me with hoary maritime stories of shipwrecks and strandings. In my fevered imagination, I was *The Flying Dutchman*, condemned to sail endlessly into the storm, and I began to cry.

"Stop yer blubbin'!"

From the corner of my eye, I saw a blood-drenched face like some old pirate from one of Grumpus's tales.

“Keep steering while I bind this. Eyes fore!”

I heard a tearing sound and shortly afterwards Grumpus took back control of the boat. He looked a grisly sight with the blood-stained sleeve of his shirt tied tightly across his wound, but in minutes he had us heading for land, driven on by the raging storm.

Grumpus never wavered until we were back at the dock, though he tottered as he stepped onto its boards. I followed him and he turned to put his hand on my shoulder.

“You did well there, lad,” he said. “You can come out with me in future.”

It was one of the few compliments I ever had from my grandfather, but it meant the world to me.

The jetty still jutted out beyond the former boat house, gently rotting away into the briny. I felt no desire to see it, but I did imagine my Grumpus with his bandaged head and his calloused hand on my shoulder.

I turned and said to him, “To thine own self be true, you used to say. Did you know you were quoting Shakespeare I wonder?Thank you, Grumpus, for being focused, determined, resourceful, tough and true to yourself. I try to follow you in those ways. But do you know why some guys have all the luck? It’s because they appreciate what they’ve got.”

THE END

Acknowledgements and Permissions

A lot of people have helped me to get this book across the finishing line. Great thanks to the friends who put a lot of time into reading and rereading the story as it grew for their encouragement and advice: Jess Gillison (and her husband Keith), Richard Lawton and Derek Wood. I also appreciate the invaluable support from Norman Howens, Lou Thorley, Ken Way and Pablo Lloyd. Also, thanks to Ken Hodgson for advice on places in and around Manchester.

Nicola Hodgson of Root and Branch Editing has been fantastic. Her incisive advice, wise counsel and positive feedback have made a huge difference. The perfect proofreading was also appreciated.

Ken Dawson of Creative Covers was wonderful to work with. As well as his work ethic and talent he has a great way of patiently teasing out what you need on the cover of your precious work. Thanks to him also for impeccable typesetting and much-needed guidance around Amazon publishing procedures. A true collaborator.

Lyrics from 'Underneath the Stars' by Kate Rusby are quoted with one time permission from Pure Records. If you haven't heard Kate's music, you should!

Author's Notes

Thank you for reading *All The Luck*. I hope you enjoyed it. If you did, I hope you will consider leaving a 5-star review for this book on Amazon. These are incredibly important for new authors!

What Came Before

Just before starting *All The Luck*, I wrote a short story titled 'Woman and Superwoman'. It was the enthusiastic reaction from those who read it that encouraged me to keep writing! If you would like to read 'Woman and Superwoman' please email me at mckee.kevin1@icloud.com and I will send you a copy. Any questions about *All The Luck* or my writing in general are also welcome and I will do my best to answer them.

What Comes Next

Coming next year will be *A Gleam Into Darkness*. In it, a witch from another world comes to Earth on a mission to save it from disaster. Can she overcome an enemy that lurks in the shadows by enlisting the help of a hero who may be only a myth?

Printed in Great Britain
by Amazon

42210940R00108